Series editor: Allan Cameron

www.vagabondvoices.co.uk/think-in-translation

Nakedness

by Sigmunds Skujiņš

translated by Uldis Balodis

Vagabond Voices
Glasgow

The publisher acknowledges subsidy towards
the translation, publication and marketing from
the Latvian Ministry of Culture and the
Latvian Writers' Union

Latvijas Rakstnieku savienība

Kultūras ministrija

For further information on Vagabond Voices, see the website,
www.vagabondvoices.co.uk

Nakedness

It's strange – she'd never slipped in a single word about the house she was living in or even which floor she was on, or the view outside her window. This thought surprised him, but only passed through his mind incidentally, just a "by the way". What stuck in his mind was his worry; his thoughts jumping around chaotically, scattering every which way like beads from a broken necklace.

There were four doors on every floor along the stairwell, which meant that Flat 15 had to be on the fourth floor. Best to climb slowly, no need to rush – the most important thing was to keep calm. He was most put off by his embarrassing habit of blushing when he felt flustered; he could feel the heat from the blood surging into his face, and it would usually seem to him that his ears had become giant and heavy like the red velvet curtains at the opera. Aware of his absurd appearance, he'd grow even more flustered, and the thought about his ears would stick in his brain; he couldn't free himself of it. That kind of debacle occurring at the first meeting would be a real catastrophe.

It was also strange that despite his discomfort, Marika's image remained very clear to him; it seemed to exist in a spot in his mind reserved just for it, like a picture cut out of a magazine placed on a blank screen. For example, he didn't know anything about these stairs that she ran up and down every day, and it was the same with Flat 15 on the fourth floor, where she would wake up in the morning and lie down to sleep in the evening, where she would iron her dresses, gaze into the mirror, write and read her letters. Only in one letter did she mention in passing that four girls live in the room. Admittedly, he had imagined the dorm a bit differently – with a long corridor and many white doors on all sides with an old, curious watchwoman and a box for hanging keys at the door, but instead this was a normal block of flats, an excellent example of how architectural styles can come together. It may not have occurred to her to describe such a place. No matter, all would become clear in a moment. The main thing was to keep his cool.

Keeping his nervousness in check, he recalled Marika's last letter, which he'd received two days before his long journey home. He would repeat every word, having reread the letter many times on the train, as though he were trying to convince himself of its contents. Maybe he did it because he was bored, but to be honest he was probably just impatient and reeling from his new freedom, all of which launched him into a kind of feverish mix of joy, longing, and hope.

Dear Sandris,

As to the question of what it is that I'm doing, it's possible to answer very simply: as always – I'm waiting. Everything that's happening right now is only temporary, without any real value or significance. In moments when it's difficult, I think about you, reread your letters, and gain new strength.

The bird cherries are blooming, I'm putting a small sprig in this envelope, though I don't know whether it will still have any scent when you receive it. The days are still hot and the blossoms are already falling from the trees. It was especially hot on Sunday. Old Mārtiņš, the kvass salesman by the station, kept on sighing, "It's hellish, like an oven, I'll have to cut the ends off my trousers." I was working the evening shift and there was a trade-union meeting afterwards. Coming from work I went to check right away whether there was a letter from you, but there wasn't. I got terribly sad, I couldn't fall asleep for a long time, later on I must have dozed off, but I jerked awake terrified in the middle of the night, thinking about how for a second week I haven't received a single line from you. Even so, I'm continuing to write to you the same as always, because then it feels like time passes quicker, bringing the moment closer that I'm awaiting with such fear and such hope.

4

Without a doubt, he was in a much better position, being able to prepare and consider everything in advance. Marika had no idea: *what if I catch her naked or, let's say, with rollers in her hair?* Maybe dropping in this way was a little sneaky? Maybe it would have been better to send a telegram from Riga – give her enough warning so that she could still manage to get through the line at the salon or at least put on some nice lipstick. And what if she's not at home? That can't be ruled out – the first shift goes from seven until two.

He anxiously inspected his reflection in the windowpane and stroked his cheeks. His chin was smooth as a whetstone. Only his short hair was stubbornly unruly; when he wet it, it dried before he could comb it, but he couldn't do anything about it now. And his suit fitted well enough, but as he was used to wearing a uniform he felt like everything around him was fluttering and flapping: the suit jacket's corners, the buttons' loose fit at his chest, his collar's long lapels.

On the steps at the third floor sat a girl who had stuffed herself into a thin calico dress – round cheeks, round breasts, round knees. She was chewing loudly on sweeties and reading a book. He was about to push past her when the girl rose up unexpectedly and examined him with a cool, unsettling stare.

"Excuse me…" he murmured.

The girl didn't answer.

"Flat 15 is still further up?"

"Yes."

"Thank you."

"You're going to Flat 15?"

"Yes."

Looking back over his shoulder, he saw that the girl was still studying him. A smell of fried fish was coming from somewhere. Golden dust motes were dancing in the sunbeams and flies darted about, buzzing as if singing.

Here… in the process of drying out, the door jamb had contracted and a gap had formed between the brick and wood. The handle hung limply as if dislocated. He must have

5

knocked too loudly, because the echo in the quiet stairwell ricocheted all the way down to the bottom. Everything fell silent on the other side of the door, no one came to open it.

"Don't waste your energy," the girl called from the third floor. "There's no one there. I've already pounded on it."

"At number 15?"

"Of course. Who'd sit inside on a day like this? The girls have run off to the riverside. Maybe you've got a key?"

"A key?"

"Never mind. That's my room too and I can't get into it either."

"No, I don't have a key."

"Well at least a knife. We could try to prise it open."

"Too bad, but even if we did, I'm no expert in picking locks."

"I am. If only there were a knife."

A light flashed in the gap after all; possibly a door had opened within the flat. He thought he heard steps. He knocked again.

"Who's there?"

The question wasn't spoken too kindly, but the voice sounded pleasant. It's possible it was Marika. He nearly recited his first and last name but caught himself at the last moment – he didn't want to appear too well behaved. Was that how Aleksandrs Draiska was supposed to come onstage, the poet and seasoned adventurer who would burst through any wall like an armoured tank?

"Who's there?"

"It's not worth saying, you wouldn't believe me anyway."

"Don't fool around."

"Honestly."

"What do you need?"

"Just a moment of your attention. Does Marika Vītiņa live here?"

"Wait."

He recognised her as soon as he saw her in the twilight of the front hall. The resemblance to the photograph was surprising: the straight nose, the somewhat high forehead, the angular jaw. Only her hair colour didn't match his expectations; he thought it could be any colour, just not golden faded copper red. Wrapping herself in a short terry robe, she regarded him with suspicious curiosity, as she nudged along one of her slippers with the foot she hadn't been able to slip into it in her haste. Did Marika really not sense it yet? With every moment that he stood there, Marika's value seemed to increase whilst his weight seemed to decrease. His fired-up courage soon collapsed.

"Allow me to introduce myself: Sandris Draiska, demobilised Special Forces *Yefreytor*…"

Now everything was supposed to change in an instant. She might even fall into his arms with unexpected impetuosity. That really could happen.

Sandris! It's you! This is crazy! My goodness! And what a fool I was in not recognising you. In my wildest dreams I never could have imagined that you would be in a suit. Oh, and how I look! I'll be right there! Wait one moment! But not behind a closed door. Please come in!

Sandris, you rascal, why didn't you warn me? That's not fair. You caught me completely off guard. Look how my heart is racing…

"What do you want?"

"I've arrived."

"That's hard to deny. And will that be all?"

This was some kind of a mistake, some kind of idiotic misunderstanding. But they were so strangely similar – perhaps he was misled by the retouched, shadowy photograph. Maybe Marika has a sister, possibly even a twin sister.

"I'd like to see Marika Vītiņa."

"Then please look faster, I have to get to work."

That couldn't have been a joke. She was saying that with complete seriousness.

"You're Marika Vītiņa?"

"Do I have to show you my papers? Are you with the police?"

"No, I already said – I'm from the army."

"Extremely interesting."

"And the most interesting thing is that we should know each other. You've sent me forty-nine letters. And have received just about as many in return."

"Letters? What letters?"

"Well… in my opinion, completely normal ones."

"Then where did I send you these 'completely normal letters' to, if I may ask?"

"To the army unit."

In the front hall, buttoning his shirt, appeared a tall young man, wide in the shoulders and thin in the waist, fairly similar in appearance to him, they even had something in common in their faces and movements.

"What's going on?" the young man asked. He probably didn't feel all that comfortable.

"Come over here, Varis, listen to this unimaginable fantasy."

"Maybe you should invite this person in. It'll take a little time to figure this one out, I think." The young man looked on with a sly grin and winked. She immediately stepped back from the threshold; this movement apparently was intended as an invitation. The young man, sticking his hands into the pockets of his black bell-bottoms, let them pass, underscoring with all his behaviour that he was a bystander with no intention of interfering in their conversation. The room really did have four beds. One of these had been sloppily covered with a chequered blanket. Expensive curtains fluttered at the open window, while last season's radio-gramophone cowered shyly between suitcases piled up behind a three-doored wardrobe.

"Please sit," said Marika. Everybody stayed standing.

"So, I've written you forty-nine letters…"

He wasn't angry any more, just deeply amused. Judging by how quickly her face cleared, her harsh coldness in no way reflected her underlying nature.

"My poems were printed in the magazine *Liesma*. After

that you began to write to me. I received your last letter two weeks ago."

"Could you show me these letters?"

"Unfortunately, no. They stayed in Riga; too large a stack to carry them all around with me. But I can show you the photograph that was in the third letter. Opening his wallet, he felt Marika's stare on his fingers and purposely tried to lend his movements an indifferent quality. The conversation had turned out to be incredibly silly. To a certain extent even insulting. It had turned into a kind of exercise in making excuses: he wasn't believed, but he objected, stubbornly persisted, and tried to prove what he was saying.

"Here it is."

Marika looked first at one side of the photograph, then the other side, and shrugged.

"Truly interesting. Well, Varis, what do you have to say?"

The young man's bright, puckish cheek wasn't shining nearly as brightly as earlier.

"A pretty picture. My gut tells me that it's something I've seen before."

"So, the picture is yours?"

"I guarantee it. But I didn't send it to you. I didn't send you anything. It must have been some kind of a stupid joke."

"Very possibly. I just doubt that someone would write forty-nine letters as a joke."

"A complete mystery. Varis, what do you think?"

"Excuse me, but when did you receive this photograph?" Taking a long and careful drag on his cigarette, the young man lifted his head.

"About a year ago. No, not quite that long. The poem was published in February of last year. In winter, in any case."

"Ancient history," the young man said. "I got mine long after that."

Marika shot Varis a lightning quick look, almost like a slap to the face. "Don't be an idiot. You heard. He got the last letter two weeks ago."

"Well, then somebody's writing them."

"And gets letters in my name? Ha. Why?"

The young man pulled the cigarette pack out of his shirt pocket again.

"I guess I forgot to offer you any. Let's poison ourselves together, if it's alright with you. My gut feeling is that we've got a reason to get to know each other. Varis, Son of Tenis, Tenisons."

"Aleksandrs Draiska. Thank you, I don't smoke, I've got other vices."

Varis's eyes flashed darkly. "Oho! I guess I didn't hear you quite right. What did you say?"

"I've got other vices."

"Smoking isn't a vice... Aleksandrs Draiska... Smoking is a weakness. Sure, sure, the world is full of all kinds of strange happenings like those letters. Sometimes you have to wonder about them just like the gypsy did: dad's white, mom's black, where did the black twins come from?"

"It's a vice to brag about weaknesses," Marika added.

"I think it's an even bigger vice to hide weaknesses."

Varis's answer sounded cool and distant, but it was aimed only at Marika and lingered as long as the glance they exchanged. After that Tenisons resumed his decidedly friendly chattiness.

"I also didn't smoke in the army. And you know why? I had to quit while I was at the gasoline depot. I came for my first guard shift and the sergeant major was at my pockets right away. He threw the matches in the toilet; all I heard was the gurgle of the water. 'From this moment on you're a non-smoker,' he said. 'It's not possible to quit smoking that easily,' I tried to object. 'A real soldier can do anything,' the sergeant major replied. 'I, for example, have quit smoking thirty-five times already.'"

"That's from Mark Twain."

"Could be. Our sergeant major knew his literature. Yeah, military service – what a strange thing. While you're assessing the wreckage, it feels like the end, but when you get home and you're living as a free man again it's nice to reminisce, don't you think?"

"You know that better than me, I haven't lived too long as a free man."

"The most important thing is to take off your uniform. And right away it feels like you've got a completely different head attached."

"For the moment I somehow don't feel it…"

Tenisons had undoubtedly shifted the conversation to army matters on purpose in order to give him a chance to understand his situation. His initial surprise gave way to disappointment, which was difficult to hide. He didn't feel so much deceived, as ashamed. He'd made a fool of himself. His entrance had been so impressive. He just hadn't foreseen one little detail – that the boards onstage might be slippery… And now he was lying flat on his back. A more perfect flop would've been impossible to imagine. Still he needed to leave with his head held high. Maybe Tenisons, out of a sense of old army boy solidarity, was trying to make his retreat easier for him, diluting any uncomfortable talk with jokes and innocent chit-chat. On the other hand, that seemed completely incomprehensible, because in this situation they were almost competitors. Maybe Tenisons was just playing a role in front of Marika, faking immunity to foolish tendencies like jealousy. In truth they'd completely switched roles. Marika became increasingly friendly; Tenisons was keeping the conversation going, but now the suspicious and careful one was him.

"So you're from Riga?" asked Tenisons.

"Yeah… kind of."

"Where are you staying? I mean, here?"

"Nowhere. I'm going back on the next train."

"That wouldn't make a lot of sense. If I were you, I'd stay in Randava, at least until Sunday night."

"Why?"

"For various reasons. First of all, because during the

summer it's pretty dumb to return to Riga on a Friday night. Second – out of curiosity – what if he, I mean the letter writer, shows up?"

"You meant to say 'she'," Marika corrected him.

"Well, let's assume, 'she'," Tenisons kept a steely calm. "And, third, because it's important never to hurry too much. Especially if there are dealings with women."

"Nevertheless, I think I'll go."

"If I were you, I'd stay… Aleksandrs Draiska. Really, I'd stay. At least until Sunday night. Right, Marika?"

"Why not? Randava is a nice town."

Through the thin door voices became audible in the stairwell. A moment later this was followed by forceful knocking and a head sticking partway into the front hall asking with exaggerated politeness, "May we come in?" After this prelude, the room's narrowness was suddenly expanded by the energy of three individuals completely unlike each other in appearance and behaviour: a lithe, chatty, dark-haired girl who was extremely pretty, as though from a fashion magazine, a short, squat, but fairly burly tomboy, and an awkwardly blushing schoolgirl with pigtails.

"Well, look how wonderful," said Marika, "the cabin crew is in full attendance."

"A complete set plus a few odd pieces." The lithe one flashed her painted eyes mischievously, without even pretending to hide her interest.

"Yes, we have a guest. May I present: Aleksandrs Draiska, a retired Special Forces *Yefreytor*. Did I get that right?"

"It's like you read it straight out of a book."

"Very pleased to meet you," the dark-haired girl theatrically extended her hand as if expecting it to be kissed. "KK. Kamita Kancāne."

Pigtails blushed even brighter and quietly murmured, "Biruta."

The tomboy stared and barked gruffly, "Caune."

"Maybe one of you knows Aleksandrs?" Tenisons beamed his sly Cheshire cat smile.

"In what way?" replied Kamita.

Tenisons didn't respond right away, but kept watching the girls. They all looked surprised.

"He writes poems. And publishes them in the magazine *Liesma.*"

"Really? How thrilling!" Kamita squeezed her arms into her hips and pushing up her breasts stood directly across from him. "Can you imagine, I've never even seen a real live poet. Last autumn there was one giving a reading at the Culture Hall, but back then I just happened to have a shift at work and so couldn't be there. And do you know what he said about himself at his reading: *I'm a potato blossom.* Isn't that amazing? A potato blossom with black, kinked hair. We don't even have a variety like that here in Randava. Tell me, are you unique in any way?"

"In terms of agriculture?"

"Well – like Čaks or Pushkin. With all kinds of focuses…"

"I don't really think so. I'm just a typical beginner."

"What's 'typical' supposed to mean? A poet can't be typical. If that were true, you'd find poets everywhere. Even in Randava."

"Kamita, you're incredibly wrong if you think that there aren't any poets in Randava."

Caune settled on to the edge of the bed and was rocking her knees back and forth rhythmically. "Ruskulis works in the Communist Party Executive Committee and the cleaner at the Invalid Centre also writes. If you want to know."

"Ruskulis?" Kamita interjected laughing. "That acne-covered slob. I'm going to faint! That, my dear, is no potato blossom. That's potatoes mashed in a pair of pants."

"But I remember your poems." Biruta shot him a look and then quickly shied away, flustered, then immediately drew closer to him again, already more secure, with a kind of spitefulness. "One of them is called 'A Flight into Dawn'. Another was about a soldier who rested for a moment on the firing range, lying down in the grass, watching a movie about home in the clouds."

"…An old movie, already watched a thousand times.
A movie that cuts out after the order 'Get up!'…

"And after that," Biruta continued, "I think it was about a girl, one whom you're expecting a letter from."

"And, and, how did it go on? Come on, Mr Author, don't leave us hanging," Kamita said imposingly.

"Does it really matter? I can't remember."

"Your poem?"

"I've filled about seven binders with my writing."

"That wouldn't even be the greatest misfortune." Tenisons clenched his face into a theatrical grimace. "The worst is that our poet is insulting us all by leaving. On the next train…"

"Well, that's just not going to happen," Kamita's voice resounded with both indignation and unshakeable conviction. "We won't let anyone slander our noble Randava. Even more so because tomorrow is my birthday. Assume that in honour of this solemn event, the schedule has been changed and all of the trains from Randava have been cancelled."

"I'll be with you in spirit."

"I fear that your spirit isn't a particularly good dance partner."

"On the other hand, it would never step on your toes."

Biruta seemed to still be trying to remember the lines of the poem.

"And you're really already leaving us?" she said. "How sad, you must have had some important errand in Randava. Maybe you came to tour our factory?"

"No, no particular reason. I just wanted to go for a ride. I hadn't been on a train in a long time."

"You're not telling the truth. You're trying to seem light-hearted, but actually you're embittered, it's easy to tell."

"Well, then don't interrogate this person like you're the police commissioner," Caune said snidely, staring at the ceiling. "As if you always only told the truth. Apparently, there's a reason. And really you shouldn't become obsessed, that's so provincial of you."

"No matter," Kamita didn't relent, "we're not letting you go. Don't forget that tomorrow night at seven you have to be at the lifeguard station on the Gauja riverside. The celebration will take place outside and will start precisely on time. Will you be there?"

"No."

"Thank you. It's all clear. So – we'll expect you."

Having escaped the room, he breathed a sigh of relief, realising somewhat hazily that despite everything he had come out of that situation almost intact – like a drowning man who'd at the last moment managed to pull himself out of the water on to the safety of the shore, still woozy from all of the water he'd swallowed, standing there now with shaking legs. He'd felt something similar only in high school after the final exam in chemistry. Now it was best not think about any of it. It was over and done with. He'd got out of there. And the door behind him was closed. How wonderful! Even if his ears were still burning.

Running down the stairs was pleasant and even relaxing in a way, his legs moving without him having to force them. He flowed like water from a sluice gate that had suddenly been opened. But maybe he was just running away, still not feeling entirely safe?

The girl from earlier was standing on the landing by the window. She still hadn't gotten inside. Horrible! The moment when he'd come up the stairs belonged to a past so distant that it had already evaporated from his awareness. Poor thing, she must have decided to wait there until she went grey.

"The ladies are still at the river?"

It seemed rude to go by without saying something, if only because they had spoken earlier. No, now everything was perfectly alright. He was bounding athletically, jauntily; he smiled a little, made a little joke… Sure, she'd probably heard the blabbering start to his conversation with Marika.

"Of course. And I'm almost done with the book, too. Did you meet her?"

"Well, I found out about her."

"But I lied. Sometimes I lie by accident…"

"Eh, a trifle. No matter. A joke's a joke. I can give you the short version fit for the newspapers, if you like."

"Thank you. I've only got time for crime novels."

"Really?"

"Yes. They're interesting to read and most importantly – they always have a happy ending. All the mysteries are solved, all the guilty are revealed."

"Then I can't help you."

"Maybe you'd like to try?"

"To read crime novels?"

"To help."

She emphatically turned the window handle and pulled open both sides.

"See, the balcony door is open…"

He instinctively looked down. There was a grassy patch overgrown with weeds and a flower bed lined with white-washed bricks. It wasn't too far of a drop, but still daunting enough.

"The key should be on the table. Will you try?" The girl's voice sounded challenging yet disinterested, as if she were asking him to take a suitcase down from a shelf or some other insignificant thing.

"To climb up on to the balcony?!"

Was she serious? Of course, it wasn't impossible. The ledge seemed wide enough. *Yeah, just one moment, it's nothing.* And how wonderful it would feel to wave to her from the balcony; nimbly grasping the railing, a dashing leap – and he was already in the room… To say no would be repugnant. But to just take a risk like that… If it were, let's say, as a bet, then it would at least make sense…

"Of course you won't climb up."

"I was just thinking whether it's worth it…"

"Worth it? I'm not planning on paying you. But you're not from around here; that was clear from the start."

16

"How do you mean?"

"You think too much. And most importantly – you don't know how to get on to a balcony at a girls' dorm. See, you have to do it like this."

She leaned out the window and threw her book up on to the balcony. After that, she deftly pulled off her slippers and threw those up there too. The calico dress was hiked up, her round limbs flashed by, white pants, and then she was standing on the ledge. It all happened so fast that he didn't manage to fully comprehend it. For a moment he choked: he'd been planning on holding her hand. But there had been no point. From below a clipped call sounded: "Look where Lība is! Watch it, crazy girl!"

She lifted her gaze and gathered her belongings from the balcony.

"Well, you saw – simple, right?"

"Yes… Almost like at the circus. You've got a talent."

But silently he thought to himself: she's crazy, completely crazy.

And he ran down the stairs listening to the rhythmic clatter of his own steps.

2

His greatest obstacle was his thoughts that stumbled and stammered, and he had to confront them again and again. His best thoughts always came five minutes too late. And maybe that's why he liked writing letters, because every sentence could be calmly sifted, reviewed, patched up, and honed. In direct conversation, eye to eye, he typically tripped himself up, and in that state of confusion he would stammer out the kind of foolishness that made him want to die of shame. Later on when he could go over his thoughts in peace, he'd find the right words as well as the right tone and the requisite degree of wit. Yes, later on – that's when he'd engage in brilliant dialogues in his mind, fencing with his words like Fanfan la Tulipe and trading his unpleasant memories for colourful fantasies. *It was just on the tip of my tongue. That's what I'd wanted to say.*

Another problem was that he gave up too easily, retreated too quickly.

The railroad station was not close to the centre of town. The meadows, riverbanks and small family gardens which had once filled these outskirts were now boasting white, fresh-baked five-storey residential buildings. Over time the old concrete belt lining the highway had become worn and twisted; long ago it had transformed from a public utility into a monument to the past. Battered dump trucks rattled and clattered back and forth. Determined grey-haired old ladies rode by on sputtering motorbikes. Dust rose and the sun beat down. The side of the road, the bushes and trees all looked like they had been covered with a scattering of grey powdered cement. Brightly coloured posters on each street corner advertised cinema shows and guest performances by Riga theatre groups. Shop windows offered groceries, consumer goods, bread. In Latvian. In Russian.

In the station square, several queues continuously alternated between growing and shrinking in length – at the bus stop, at the kvass barrel, at the ice cream stand.

The waiting rooms were permeated by twilight and pleasant coolness. He glanced at the schedule, the next train to Riga left at 2:20 p.m.

Why had Tenisons tried to convince him to stay in Randava until Sunday night? He had to have some kind of angle – that guy seemed crafty. His kindness, at any rate, was fairly suspicious. And then those strange looks that Tenisons would shoot at Marika. Did she really not know anything or was she just pretending? The photograph was real. But Marika didn't even seem especially surprised. It was almost like she was Brigitte Bardot, whose likeness is produced by the thousands and sold in every kiosk.

The station platform was empty and bare. A long freight train sat on the siding. Logs clanked rhythmically as they were tossed out of the rail cars. He walked around the station building and out again into the square. The asphalt had warmed in the sun and was soft under the soles of his shoes. The line at the kvass barrel had grown longer; people were standing with bottles, jugs and jars. The attendant, a wizened old man in a white overcoat, with rolled-up trouser legs and large wooden clogs, was doing his work with the patience of a saint. It had to be Mārtiņš. Another acquaintance he'd never met. Something was pushing him closer to this man, and it didn't feel like thirst.

"Mārtiņš, pour faster, I don't have time to wait."

"Faster, faster. Every task, my dear girl, has to be done carefully and well. Do you also rush a barber?"

"I can't even get to a barber."

"Grow out some braids, just like girls did in the old days. Back in the day, there was just one ladies' hair salon and even that one was always half-empty."

"Back then, my friend, there was no textile factory here. There were three thousand fewer women's heads here. And when Phase 2 opens, there will be another three thousand."

19

"Well, how much should I pour?"

"Four litres."

"Good. It's important to drink a lot, especially in the second half of your life. Otherwise a person dries out like an old piece of leather. And all the bad parts don't get rinsed out. I saw a big article on it in *Health* magazine."

There was change sitting in a dish close to the spigot, soaking in kvass.

"Well, how much should I pour?" Mārtiņš asked him.

"One large," he answered when his turn came.

"You must be from the army?" Mārtiņš carefully studied him from head to toe as he rinsed out a glass.

"Is that what I look like?"

"That's what I'm seeing. A kind of Sunday school face. It's obvious right away, a person ho hasn't put down any roots yet. Someone in no hurry, without worries. And anyway, from where else would a young guy suddenly appear in Randava?"

Other people standing in line were also starting to pay attention to him.

"So, do you know everybody?"

"I'd like to think I almost do. With the girls it's a little tougher. They buzz around here like mosquitoes on Midsummer's day. But there are just a few young guys in Randava. And no more than two kvass barrels, one in the centre, the other with old Mārtiņš. Do you want some more?"

"No, thanks."

He put down the empty glass and started to walk away, but then after a short distance turned around and came back.

"Could you tell me where Priežu Street is?"

"Priežu Street? Do you know where the bus station is? Well, it's right by that. Up over there, near the river. And then turn left immediately. It's a bit narrow."

"Thanks."

He'd given up too quickly, retreated too fast.

There was also another address: Priežu Street 8. Not really

another one, but maybe the most important one. The train wasn't leaving until 2:20 p.m.

He was more familiar with the centre of town in Randava and remembered its different parts from years ago: the large square, the hotel, the theatre, the old church. Before his military service when his father was still alive, they'd go for a drive almost every Sunday, most often to northern Vidzeme, where his father felt he was from, even though he'd lived most of his life in Riga.[1]

The outskirts of Randava were new to him. Countless family homes were hiding behind carefully manicured trees and yards down labyrinths of small, sandy streets. Apparently, these had been built right after the war when the town centre was still in ruins. Back then many cities resembled old burned-out oak trees – their centres empty and blackened, with only their outer layers and bark continuing to cling to life.

Chickens clucking, dogs barking, the smell of jasmine blossoms but also barnyard. Lazy, snoozing cats. Fruit trees covered with netting. Garages and sheds. Satellite TV receivers resembling radar dishes sitting on tall masts.

"Is this Priežu Street 8?"

"Of course. What do you want?"

A tall, gaunt woman slowly stood up from a strawberry patch and brushed off her knotted arthritic fingers. She studied him with eyes half closed against the sunlight, her chest heaving as she breathed in and out heavily.

"I have a bit of a question… Actually a fairly long story. You see, I've sent letters to this address, it was given to me, letters sent to the dorm sometimes go missing…"

"Uh-huh," the woman responded. Her eyes became more lively, her lips drew into a barely noticeable smile. "Then you're him…"

---

1   Latvia is traditionally divided into four regions: Kurzeme, Zemgale, Vidzeme and Latgale. Vidzeme is located east of the Gulf of Riga and north of the Daugava River in the north-central part of Latvia.

"Exactly. My name is Aleksandrs Draiska."

"Of course, of course. They came every week. Sometimes even two a week. Those soldiers, they love to write. When my nephew was in the army, he also wrote letters."

"Could you tell me who got them?"

"Your letters, right?"

"Yes."

"Whomever you sent them to was the one who got them. I didn't keep them. My goodness, it couldn't be any other way. I didn't have any part in it. They asked me and of course I let them. I've got no problem with them using my mailbox. Why not help people out?"

"That's all fine. Thank you so much! I didn't mean to insinuate anything. I just wanted to ask if you knew her…"

"Who then?"

"Well, her, the one who got the letters."

"How could I not know her? She always bought cottage cheese from me at the market. Sort of chatty, full of energy."

"What's her name?"

The woman dropped her hands, sighed and shot him a pity-filled look.

"Well, who do you think? Marika Vītiņa, or whoever it was. Don't you know who you scribbled all those notes to? I was actually quite happy about it, you had such nice handwriting."

"Could you tell me, please, what colour is her hair?"

"I've got too much to do to keep track of hair colour. Maybe brown, maybe yellow – who can even say? Nowadays everybody's bleaching their hair, colouring it, whatever they come up with."

"Maybe red?"

"It could be purple, for all I care. It doesn't matter to me."

The conversation was beginning to annoy the woman. She didn't understand what he wanted from her and felt offended, as she struggled with the feeling that she was being accused of something. She grew sullen and angrier, but like many older people, she didn't find it easy to stop and switch directions once she'd started down a particular path.

"I don't keep track of people's hair. It's none of my business. I don't even know what colour my dead husband's hair was. She asked and I let her. I didn't really want to: every person has an address of their own, but she said…"

"That's fine. Thank you."

"Nothing's fine. If it were fine, you wouldn't come here to pump me for answers."

"No, really…"

"Tell me – and keep it short and sweet – what do you want?"

"Just one more question, the last one: where does Marika Vītiņa live?"

"You don't know that either?"

"No. But…"

"Well, that's what happens when you write to a strange address, isn't it? She lives in the dorm. On Stacijas Street. Where else? I can't remember the building number, can't ever keep numbers straight in my head."

"It's all clear now. Thanks."

All of a sudden he wanted to laugh, but he didn't know why. Nothing was clear. There was still a secret here, a tempting twist in this game that begged to be better understood. And wasn't that exactly what he wanted? Yes, but why had he come here? It was a game right from the start, the search, the hope to find her, staying hot on her trail. A mystery address, mystery handwriting, a mystery photo. Everything else was formed by his imagination. There were no facts, just a hypothesis, which only became more intriguing with every letter: one more question, just one more. Why was he treating this whole thing so seriously? Many guys would write to two, three, even ten girls all at the same time. Surprises, naturally, were part of the rules of this game. And losing tickets, too, just like in any lottery. You had to expect that.

Did Marika really not know anything? How could it be? It

didn't matter. Her name was just a code. He needed to figure out what was hiding behind that code.

But then there was still his usual faintness of heart. A silly lack of confidence. Shyness and an absence of initiative. He knew himself all too well. An unforeseen obstacle and his energy would disappear in a blink. Thank goodness, there was a reason to retreat.

When it came to school dances, he had never asked girls he actually liked. "Would it be appropriate if I went up to her at the first dance? Too obvious. She'll figure it out and know my secret right away." At age fifteen he'd write anonymous letters to the beautiful Iveta who was in his grade but in a different class. His carefully crafted letters – complete with meticulously chosen witticisms and thick with brilliant paradoxes – had produced results. Pēteris gave him up and Iveta sent him a note with an invitation to meet. He came to the agreed spot an hour early, in complete disbelief at his success. Iveta arrived and waited, but he was never able to summon up the courage to crawl out from the shadows behind the gate where he'd been hiding. The next day he wrote her another note, turning it all into a joke, mercilessly ridiculing Iveta for letting herself be fooled so easily. Just so she wouldn't know the truth.

At any rate, it couldn't have been a coincidence that the old woman had referred to Marika by name and given her address. And incidentally, he'd sent the first two letters to Flat 15 at the dorm. And those were received.

Besides, what was waiting for him in Riga? He'd said he'd be leaving on the next train – that sounded impressive. But why?

He glanced at his watch and started walking back towards the centre of town. But at no time did he feel like the poet Aleksandrs Draiska or the detective Sherlock Holmes.

3

The hotel was located between the old Livonian Order castle ruins and the theatre. There had once been a restaurant there on the bottom floor where he and his father had often had lunch.

At home in a yellowing pre-war magazine sat a description of his father – "a young, capable scientist". Looking back at him from the photograph was a thin, elegant person with thick hair, hiding half his face behind large, black spectacles of the kind that Harold Lloyd used to wear, according to the article. The father who lived in his memories had nothing in common with this delicate dandy. He knew a stooping, heavy man with wide shoulders and rough workman's hands. His round forehead was now adorned only at the temples with a few shocks of grey; his father never complained about his eyesight and used glasses only for reading. This doctor of science cooked, went shopping at the market, used a vacuum cleaner. His mother was twenty years younger than his father.

When he was born, his father was already forty-four. He was doted over, protected, and pampered like a little Dalai Lama. His nanny would check every toy first for sharp edges. He wasn't allowed to walk down the stairs on his own. A special screen was placed in front of the window, so he wouldn't fall out. He wasn't allowed to go out into the yard, because there were "rowdy boys" there.

He learned to read very early, with books standing in for toys, friends, and to a certain extent even movement. That summer when his mother was living in the south, he almost never left the summer cottage – he just ate, slept and read: at age ten he weighed forty-seven kilograms. At school he was nicknamed Bouillon.

His attachment to his father, which had at first been just instinctive, grew even stronger when accompanied by a mind and desire characteristic of adolescent psychology to weigh and judge everything for oneself. Love was supplemented by wonder, respect and friendship. His father never forced anything on him, nor did he pour his knowledge on to him in a depressing, suffocating stream like frozen earth from an excavator's scoop. His father was sensitive and understanding without any prejudice against the unusual; he had this wonderful sense of existing on equal footing with all living things. His knowledge seemed endless, perhaps precisely because he didn't limit it with lines or parentheses, but instead tried to learn more about every possible topic in order to uncover not only his own erudition, but also his ignorance. He had a sharp, all-encompassing view and the ability to express a realisation in precisely the form that it had shot into his mind or, as he himself said, while the thoughts were alive and hadn't lost their freshness.

Now the restaurant was, it appeared, in the new supermarket building and the hotel took up its bottom floor. The woman on duty, who was dressed in a white smock, was hiding in a small cell which was reminiscent of a movie theatre ticket booth. The window was closed and she was speaking to someone on the telephone. Another woman, also in a white smock, was sitting on the couch drinking a bottle of kefir. A plastic loudspeaker was explaining in whispered tones what parents had to do in order to cultivate a sense of practicality and love of work in their children. Finally, the window opened.

"Excuse me, is there any place to stay the night in Randava?"

"No."

"Just a bed would be fine."

"Full up to the roof."

"Even just a couple of chairs."

"No place to put them, young man."

"That's impossible. In a giant barn like this."

"Then you don't know what's going on in our town. Last night, for example, twenty-two girls arrived. The new dormitory building isn't finished yet…"

The one who was drinking kefir put her bottle down and wiped away the white moustache above her upper lip with her palm.

"It would be different if you were a girl. Then we could still put you up somewhere. But right now everything is full of girls. More than ten are scheduled again for tomorrow."

"Wow! Where are they all coming from?"

"From all over the place. From Daugavpils, from Ventspils, from Joniškis. Most of all though from Belarus. There's good pay at the plant."

The woman on duty looked over at him and smiled mischievously. "Only young and pretty ones. What a selection…"

"Uh-huh. Who'd have thought it."

"Live a while with us and you'll start to think…"

"But there isn't anywhere to live."

"That's true. There's nowhere to live, but somehow everybody's still living."

The woman on duty had finished playing with her keys and, picking up the telephone receiver again, began to dial a number.

"Come by around eight in the evening," she said, her voice noticeably softening. "The auditor of the consumers' cooperative is planning on leaving. It may be that you'll get lucky."

He came out of the hostel and stopped, unable to decide right away on his next course of action. *Well, figure out what you're going to do, make a decision and then act on it; you're a free man.* Everything turns out to be so damn complicated: to stay, to go, to give up, to try to figure it out… Up until now, others had made the most important decisions for him: at home it had been his father, at school his teachers and in the army his commanders. A free man… honestly, this was a new situation for him. And right away a pretty lousy one. But it's possible that he just wasn't used to it yet.

The sun's heat weighed like a heavy burden on the shoulders of his dark jacket. There was no sense in standing in front of the hostel. He walked into the old park surrounding the castle ruins, dragging himself down the steep hillside all the way to the Gauja.

In the evening this place would surely be teeming with romantically minded couples, but right at this moment it felt heavy with an almost uncomfortable peacefulness. Not a single living soul. On the gravelled paths flashes of the sun's silvery reflection quietly flickered through the green canopy formed by the trees. Shadowy corners covered in ferns breathed out coolness and the scent of wet earth. Openings hidden among the bushes. Benches. Tables fashioned from old, heavy millstones.

His watch showed it was half past one, and he still hadn't really had any breakfast. His stomach was contorted with ravenous hunger. He could go and eat lunch at least. This thought resonated agreeably with memories of his earlier visits to Randava with his father.

Happy that he didn't need to wander around aimlessly any longer, he quickened his step and, having returned to the square by the shortest path, he went straight to the new supermarket.

Only then did he notice that there truly was a noticeably large number of girls in the town. On the street, at the bus stop, everywhere. Just like soldiers on leave, they rarely went anywhere on their own, but stuck together in small groups. They gazed out confidently, talked to each other loudly and laughed. Most of them really were good-looking, dressed and styled according to the latest fashions. Painted toenails, coloured eyelids. This weather-beaten country town had really progressed.

The store further brightened his mood. Between the striking girls in Randava and the new supermarket there definitely was some kind of order here. There couldn't be the slightest doubt about that. This wasn't some kind of provincial country store any more, which sold cotton quilted jackets, rubber boots and saddle straps. Even the smell of the store was different – soft and refined in a feminine way.

Nylon and silk bubbled up from the dazzling display cases. The salesgirls raised delicate undergarments, glittering vials and sparkling jewellery.

He didn't need anything at the store, but driven by curiosity he strode across both floors front to back.

The entrance to the restaurant was located next to the store. He walked looking around attentively like a hunter. His great hunger had died down. Again he felt lively and carefree, full of energy. But at the same time, for some reason, he also felt a little nervous; almost as if he was waiting for, hoping to meet, or find someone.

The restaurant was comfortable, tastefully decorated, and pleasantly empty. All along the large windows stretched a balcony with an expansive view of the town square. The roof, which projected far over the edge of the building, protected the room from the sweltering sun.

He ordered quickly and to pass the time began to lightly tap a tune on the tablecloth with his fingertips. That's not polite, his mother would have told him; at the table you have to sit quietly as a person's true nature is most in evidence when they're eating... His true nature was especially rude, because at an empty table, he never knew where to put his hands. His mother's own true nature was most in evidence when she was knitting. She was like a knitter from a cowboy movie: they could be shooting off their pistols all around her, but absolutely nothing could constrain the rapid movements of her needles. She knitted dresses, sweaters, mittens, shawls, trousers, coats, hats: everything that a person could imagine. She would knit them and then quickly unravel them and knit them all over again from the beginning.

The waitress brought bread and set the table. An amazing behind, as round as a potter's wheel, and what legs. Judging from her face, probably Russian, but who knows. Anyway, she had the kind of gaze that made it seem like she didn't see anybody. And she flashed her wedding ring too much.

He crossed his arms and grimaced dejectedly, feeling a great urge just to gaze confidently and freely at the waitress's face, but wasn't nearly self-confident enough to do that.

There were two people at the next table. The younger one – diminutive, round with short arms and tiny, little hands and no neck. The hair above his furrowed brow stuck straight up. His thin, snub nose weakly supported thick glasses with cracked lenses; these kept sliding down but his straight index finger was positioned as if in warning to push them back up again. The older one, who was about twice his size, was dressed in a bright chequered shirt. The only parts of his considerable figure that were visible were his back and the chocolate-coloured nape of his neck which was haloed by a ring of white hair. They both drank beer and talked loudly.

The waitress brought their food.

"Thank you, could you bring some mustard?" Which for him was almost heroic.

Crew Cut said to Chequered Shirt, "In this case I'd like to remind you of Honoré Gabriel Riqueti Mirabeau's words: 'Only fools fail to change their opinions.'"

"Mirabeau was a certified idiot and always found himself starved of money. You can't just accept any words uttered whilst starving for money."

"Idiocy, just like starving for money, is a relative concept."

"War has always been awful, but people have always fought wars. Why? We don't know. Why do people laugh, why do they dream? Clearly, there's some kind of a cog built into our machinery that moves it all."

"Forgive me, but as a biologist I can't really agree with you. Humanity has learned to do many things which don't correspond at all to our natural programming. Reason, I would venture, corrects the laws of nature. The chemist, pharmacist, scientist and doctor, David Hieronymus Grindel, who descends from the Grunduļi clan, an ancient Latvian family of mast-wrights, has made some very interesting statements in this regard…"[2]

"Reason… I have to laugh. Scratch that thin layer of reason with your fingernail and from a tiny Size 44 man, 44,000 devils will appear."

"Bravo, that's good! I'll remember that."

"One shouldn't idealise the progress of humanity. The gramophone with its horn already seems like a laughably prehistoric relic, but *Hamlet* could have been written even today…"

This dialogue attracted his attention. He must have also turned his chair a little in the direction of the quarrellers. It's not polite to eavesdrop on the conversations of others, but sometimes it's too interesting not to. Nobody knows him here or has ever seen him, nor will likely run into him in the future.

The waitress returned empty-handed. "You probably won't need mustard," she said in clear Latvian with only a slight hint of an accent.

"No," said the younger one.

It appeared there was no mustard in the kitchen. After looking around, he approached the two beer drinkers.

The older one, tracking the mustard jar with his eyes, turned his head. And suddenly catching sight of him slammed his palm down on the edge of the table.

"Oh, Kaspars! Vilis's son!"

That came so unexpectedly that he was completely dumbfounded.

"Well, am I not right? Didn't I guess?"

"To a certain extent… possibly."

"Not 'to a certain extent', but completely seriously. Your father was my best friend. There's not a lake in Latvia where

2   *Mast-wrights* were tradesmen who selected and processed the logs used for constructing ship masts, crossbeams for ship sails, and also windmill sails. At the height of this trade, the mast-wright families were among the wealthiest Latvian families in Riga.

31

we haven't been fishing. Vilis and I and also the late painter Jānis Bromalts. You probably don't remember me?"

"Not really. Well, maybe just a little bit. Like in a fog."

"But I carried you around piggyback in Ikšķile. You had little white patent leather boots with red tips."

He said this in the same tone that one would hear an indictment read in court.

"Very possibly."

"Once we caught some crayfish but, while we were drinking vodka in the kitchen, you poured them all into the well. Do you remember?"

"That I remember."

"I recognised you right away. Vilis's copy."

Old Aparjods in the flesh. His face had appeared in schoolbooks, newspapers, magazines, encyclopaedias. And he had to end up here, as if there were no other places to eat in Randava.

Aparjods got up, pushed back his chair and, staggering like a sailor, with his stomach stuck out, walked round the table. The younger one also moved closer while remaining behind his neighbour's back. It just wasn't possible to stay seated any more.

"Roberts Aparjods," the professor extended his hand.

"Pleased to meet you. I, however, of course, you…"

"But my name is Kalniņš," Crew Cut bowed quickly. "You may not end up remembering that. Kalniņš is a common surname in Latvian. So to be more specific, I'm Gatiņš from the Randava jail."

"That's not right," Aparjods corrected him, "he's blabbering. Not from the jail, but from the secondary school at the local prison for minors. As you can see, even in the slammer nobody's safe from questionable students."

"I think, some reorganisation efforts need to be undertaken," said Gatiņš. "In the way of communication. Excuse me, this table has only three seats."

"Of course," Aparjods's domineering gesture had already

dismissed all possible objections. "Ņina! Where are you, sinful child? Move this youngster over to us."

"I don't know… That would probably be a wasted effort. I'm really in a hurry…"

"It would be rude if we each were to sit at their own table. Your father was my friend. We especially enjoyed visiting verdant Rampūzītis. The breams that came out of there were like shovels. In a few hours, we'd have a bucketful of the fattest eels. As I said, 'In Latvia there is no lake…'"

"Sure, sure Chief, one shouldn't exaggerate," Gatiņš's eyes gleamed like a surgeon's knives behind the thick lenses of his glasses. "Latvia has 3195 lakes with a surface area larger than one hectare."

"I'm talking about real lakes, not some tadpole ponds."

"In that case, tell me – where is Lake Ķentele?"

"I've caught more fish in Lake Ķentele than some have ever seen."

"And where is Lake Šķīnūzis?"

"Lake Šķīnūzis is empty, there's nothing to see in Šķīnūzis."

"Many apologies, but this is one and the same lake."

"You can teach that to ignoramuses in school, but you'll never convince a sensible person of that. There's a river in the middle."

"Not a river, but a strait."

"Precisely a river."

"Ņina! The beer won't be enough any more. Do you have any cognac?"

"You really don't have to," he tried to object again. "Honestly, I've got no time."

"You don't have time to eat lunch? Don't make me laugh. One hour for lunch is the standard. Even those sentenced to hard labour by the tsar were given one hour. If you don't mind my asking, what are you doing in Randava that's so important?"

"It's a complicated thing. To do with documents. A friend from my military service days asked that I take care of it."

"And you're taking care of it now?"

"I arrived this morning."

"Only this morning?"

Choked sobs burst forth from Aparjods's chest: it was impossible to tell if he was coughing or laughing.

"The professor is already taking care of business in Randava for a third week," Gatiņš interjected.

"Do you still live in the same place on Rainis Boulevard?"

"The same place."

"How is your mother doing?"

"I guess alright, thank you. Like always."

"Is she working?"

"She's working."

"And you? Do you work? Are you studying? Are you taking a break?"

"I finished high school before my military service. I haven't figured anything out yet."

"You were a small tot missing his baby teeth... Damn it, how time flies! How time flies! And look, Vilis is already in the cemetery. Bromalts, too. All the decent people are already there. Wait, wait, when did Vilis actually die – in sixty-four or sixty-three?"

"Sixty-four."

"No." Aparjods was a bit off his mark as he was pouring the cognac, and missed Gatiņš's glass.

"Somehow it didn't work out. Ņina! See what happened. If you don't help us, we'll be drowning in a minute."

The waitress was completely unrecognisable. The cool, tall and unattainable beauty had become simple, nice and obediently helpful as she darted around giving Aparjods the kindest of smiles. At this shabby old man with false teeth, a bald head and clothes like a shepherd's on a collective farm. Truly amazing. Fame? Money? Hardly. There had to be some other hook.

"Thank you, Ņina," said Aparjods, "you're the best girl. Without you Randava would be hell's pantry."

The professor removed the flower from Gatiņš's buttonhole and pinned it on Nina's little apron.

"That's an excellent flower," said Gatiņš, "grown using a special fertiliser. My sister works as an anaesthetist – on those machines for putting people to sleep."

"You couldn't use that machine for transporting fertiliser," Aparjods lifted a glass.

"Correct. But one nice day they were called to the zoo and told, 'The lion needs its nails cut, can't you just put that devil to sleep a little bit, otherwise it'll get so upset that it might have a heart attack. A slight puff of laughing gas, and it's all over and the manicure done.'"

"Just a regular odd job!"

"Sure. They just can't pay. So they think and think – and finally figure it out: dear doctor, don't you have a family garden? There is no way she doesn't have one. And now they're happy: we're giving you a truckload of lion manure, the highest-quality stuff."

"Gatiņš, don't ruin everyone's appetite."

"Why hide the truth? That flower is from my sister's garden."

"Let's raise our glasses instead."

"Inciting others to alcoholism is forbidden by law."

"I'm spurring on everyone to work."

Everyone took a drink. The talk grew louder. People began showing up at the surrounding tables.

"Hey mate, why do you look so sad?" Gatiņš laughed mischievously through his cracked lenses.

"So others don't see that I'm happy."

"Pretty original. So what are you happy about?"

"About ending up in Randava."

"Do you think you'll stay here long?"

"I don't know… Maybe until Sunday night."

4

The electric light was glowing; the sunset continued to shine brightly through the large windows. The loud clatter of the orchestra occasionally broke the stillness, drowning out every other sound like a passing train.

Some couples were dancing. Slightly inebriated men studied the few women there with hungry eyes – though mostly without causing any trouble. A disagreeably heavy dinner before sleep. The office manager with the administrative officer, and the depot director with seven employees after the trade-union meeting. Habit, obligation, weakness of character.

Their table had grown heavy with bottles and dishes of food. Aparjods had ordered it all at once. Some people were milling around and refused to leave them alone; glasses held high, they'd come up, say hello, introduce themselves, nod politely, shake hands. *Pleased to meet you! Yes, how nice. Your name was familiar to us, even if we hadn't yet made your acquaintance. We wanted to say a few words about your most recent publication...*

Next to this colourful display he seemed to fade into the background. Just an anonymous and nondescript figure among the usual group of hangers-on. On his own, worth less than nothing. Nobody knew him, nobody even asked who he was. In that sense, there was no danger, he could sit there without worrying; watch, listen, and make a mental note of anything that might be useful in the future.

Aparjods drank a lot, but you couldn't tell. Sweat covered his forehead like dew and his shrill voice became more grating. It seemed like the whirlwind of praise didn't boost his mood, but nor did it bother him. This was simply the way things had to be. This was normal. The professor didn't get involved in long conversations. He had an opinion ready on every matter. These were sharp, abrupt and unassailable. He would produce them like a card sharp produces aces – *kaboom* and *kapow* – without mercy, full of zeal. One hell of a guy.

Around midnight Gatiņš started to become restless. "My dear intelligentsia, it's time to move out into the fresh air. Like Jean-Jacques Rousseau said, 'Back to nature.' From a practical standpoint, it could be in my garden at home under the jasmine trees. Let's go."

"What are we going to do there?" Aparjods looked insepar-able from his chair, like a tree rooted in the ground.

"The same as here," Gatiņš answered. "Let's take our bottles with us. And Velta will be thrilled to give us a little snack to bite on."

"She'll be biting alright…," Aparjods retorted.

"No, that's not in my wife's character. She'll just be very surprised."

"I bet she'll be."

"She'll be pleasantly surprised."

"Woken up in the middle of the night. Don't talk nonsense."

"She won't even be asleep yet."

"Even worse."

"She might even be waiting."

"Be honest. You're afraid to show up at home by yourself."

But Gatiņš persisted and kept trying to charm Aparjods, promising all manner of tempting delights, beginning with nightingale songs and ending with porridge and fishing at daybreak on the Gauja River.

The atmosphere in the restaurant grew increasingly strange. Men embraced, sang, slapped each other on the shoulder. The large chandeliers went out, one after another. The waitresses brought the bills. The men in the orchestra slowly gathered up their instruments, but looked as if they were still waiting for something.

Gatiņš emerged from the kitchen. His legs were short, and the seat of his trousers bulged out absurdly from underneath his wrinkled jacket.

"And look, we've even got corks. Shut those bottles up and

stick them in your bags. My unfortunate friend, grab some mineral water. Not a moment to lose if we're to abandon this sinking ship."

It was unusually light outside. The sky radiated an electric blue like an aquarium illuminated by artificial light, and the town's dark silhouette of roofs, towers and countless television antennas was sharply outlined against it.

People were still walking up and down the main street: young men with guitars, processions of young women in summer clothes.

They had to wait for quite a long time for a bus to come. One finally showed up travelling from Pārgauja, but was on its way back to the depot. Gatiņš negotiated with the driver and arranged it so that he took them almost all the way home.

Further on, the road curved around freshly excavated sewage lines and alongside some giant trees. The air smelt of barns and fresh hay. The frozen silence hunted stealthily for even the smallest sound. Aeroplanes travelling above the fiery horizon inscribed the bright sky with unusual symbols.

For some reason it felt like each step had to be taken quietly and carefully, but at the same time it felt difficult not to laugh. It might make for an interesting game – one where attention and adventurous sneaking around formed only one part, which would be followed by another part – a loud, merry and passionate one.

"So," said Gatiņš, pushing open the gate, "here we are."

"Well, what are we going to do?" asked Aparjods. "Maybe climb up to the hayloft?"

"Up in the hayloft or out in the garden, it doesn't matter. But first maybe let's go inside. I have to wake up the wife."

"Whatever happens, in court we'll testify on your behalf, Gatiņš."

"Velta will be pleasantly surprised. We don't get guests like these every day."

"Let alone every night."

"Believe me. I know my own wife."

A narrow hallway filled with outdoor clothes. A hot, stuffy kitchen. Flies asleep on the white tiles. A milk separator. Pots, jugs, measuring cups. Gauze squeezed dry.

From a side room, an old-sounding woman's voice asked, "Gatiņš, is that you? Close the door. Don't shine the light in Andrītis's eyes."

"Yeah, yeah…" Gatiņš answered before turning back to his guests telling them, "Wait just a moment. Everything will be up to the highest possible standards."

"Speaking just for myself, I've got nothing to lose. My life is insured," Aparjods said, his voice full of irony.

"But I'm used to it. Commandos fight, no matter the circumstances. Wherever they're dropped. Even on the edge of a volcanic crater."

That bordered on boasting, but the words kept flowing almost as if under their own power. He wanted to talk, to talk about himself, to create something surprising, unique.

Another woman's voice could be heard now from behind the wall. It was sleepy, groaning. A child started crying and didn't stop for a long time.

There were nylons and lingerie hanging across the back of a chair. He came to a sudden stop, his delight slowly ceasing. He shouldn't have come inside. Everything he saw and heard here seemed too raw and not meant for strangers. After their carefree, open wandering, he felt like he'd run straight into a cramped, constricting fish basket. It seemed like there wasn't even enough air to breathe. A pink lampshade cast its dense, ruddy light. The window was rendered opaque by a thick cloth. A pushchair. An old-fashioned desk. One of the walls of the room was taken up by a large bookcase.

Gatiņš arrived, a little confused, with bread, onions and a large bowl of lard.

"Velta is a little tired, but that doesn't change a thing. Feel right at home."

"Hush!" Aparjods lifted a finger in warning. "Be quiet, loudmouth. No drama."

"There's nothing to worry about. It's not like this is the first time."

"Let's get out of here."

All of a sudden he froze. Was it a mistake? His imagination? Or was he already so dizzy drunk that he was starting to see things? On the desk, pinned into the letter holder, in between different kinds of papers was Marika Vītiņa's photograph. From the same series that he had in his pocket. He stumbled closer. No doubt at all. It was her.

"What's caught your interest?" asked Gatiņš.

"Hm. This photograph. Do you know her?"

"I'm forced to know her. There's nothing I can do about it."

"What does that mean?"

"Not know my own sister-in-law, that really would be something."

"What's her name?"

"Marika. Did you want to meet her? She doesn't have a boyfriend yet.."

"She really doesn't have one yet?"

"Of course she does. But, in my opinion, she's one of those girls who always keeps another one in reserve. Of course. And she's even musical."

"Really?"

"Sings in a quartet, plays the guitar."

"Where does she live?"

"Oh, I see, you've got a practical angle. That really is a sensitive point. Unfortunately, she doesn't have a flat."

"I mean her address."

"That I don't know. But don't worry, tomorrow you'll meet her at breakfast."

"Hurry up," Aparjods was growing impatient, "summer nights are short, just like life."

Mysterious, motionless shadows were outlined darkly under the trees out in the garden. A large, shaggy dog walked up quietly, panting and winding around his legs.

"Keep going, keep going," Gatiņš urged, "the best spot is beneath the jasmine tree."

"There's only one glass, so get in line if you want some refreshment. Kaspars, you're first up!"

"Thanks," he said, "I'm very sorry, but I've got to go now. It was a very nice time."

"Got to go?" Aparjods was surprised. "Where to?"

"Back to town."

"To Randava? Right away? At night?"

"Yes. I can't do anything about it. It's important. It's a good thing I remembered."

"Like a classicist from Latgale once said, 'I must be a little dumb.' Try knocking me down, it won't bother me."

"No need to advertise your own ignorance," Aparjods said harshly. "Indecisiveness is a characteristic of youth. That can't be changed. And it's clear that nobody's being kept here by force."

"This is just too shocking. Too bad, my friend, too bad. Such a terrible blow. Maybe your important work could be done tomorrow during the day?"

"No," he answered stubbornly. "I have to go. It's really good that I remembered."

"If you need to go, then you need to go. You shouldn't cancel your plans," said Aparjods. "Youngsters are crazy, of course. But once upon a time we were young too. Let him run."

Where did he suddenly get this silly idea? It was hard to imagine more naive lies than these. And then this rush that was already turning into a panic. From the outside he appeared crazy. This was the right time to leave. Meeting Marika with Aparjods around! That's all he needed! Definitely not.

However, he once again had reason to consider himself a happy person. Or perhaps a once unhappy person. Right at that moment he couldn't really say. It wasn't clear, and more importantly, it would become even less clear. That the letters were sincere, he had no doubt. But why then did Marika pretend that she didn't know anything? And, if she really didn't write them, who did?

He was walking along the highway in the direction of an old church spire that was visible above the trees in the distance. It looked like a rocket being readied for launch. The monotonous clack-clack of his shoes on the asphalt broke through the silence. Layers of fog lay across parts of the meadows. The night felt carefree after all.

It also smelt of hay here. Fields bordered by a line of gates. A large, red moon lifting itself up over the edge of the horizon.

Interesting, what time is it? Where's he going? The waiting room at the station was open all night. But what if he just crawled into the fresh hay right here? He yawned. He was incredibly tired. Honestly, he was already half asleep. He stopped and slept. Just like during manoeuvres.

5

The knocking was piercing and sounded like machine-gun fire. He knew who was at the door, but couldn't wake up. His head seemed glued to the pillow.

The sunlight was blinding. The bed next to him was made and no one was sleeping in it. Just like during the night when he'd arrived.

"Yeah, yeah, coming…"

He got up too fast and everything in front of his eyes seemed to shift position; walking to the door, he almost ran into the door jamb. Oh right, there was still one room ahead of him. And then the hallway after that. Flats. The luxury suite. What an idiotic misnomer! Why did the door need to be locked? The woman on duty had made it clear: you won't have the room to yourself, the other bed is taken.

The person who'd been knocking turned out to be, much to his great surprise, Varis Tenisons. In a white jacket. Flushed, fresh-faced, his hair trimmed short, carefully combed, and still a little wet – he had the air of a boxer.

"Good morning. Well, how did you sleep last night in Randava? Old people like to say, 'When you sleep, you've no time for sinning.' But in weather like this, it seems to me like sleeping is itself a sin."

"I'm so sorry."

"For what? The sinning?"

"For not having any trousers on."

He ran into the bathroom and quickly stuck his head under the faucet. Afterwards he vigorously dried himself off with a towel.

What was Tenisons after? Nobody bangs on a door like that without a reason. And how had he found him anyway?

"So you stayed after all?"

There was something not altogether convincing about his overly cheerful chattering; he didn't seem as happy as he was trying to look.

"It turned out that way…"

"And you made the right choice. Riga isn't going anywhere."

"Let's hope."

Varis pulled out a pack of *Elita* and, lightly tapping his fingers against it, produced two cigarettes.

"Can I offer you one?"

"Thanks, I don't smoke."

"Right, I completely forgot. For some reason, I thought that all writers smoked. At least that's how caricatures of them are always drawn. Can you tell me, have you been writing poetry for a long time?"

"Poetry? Only now and again."

"What's your main line then?"

"What do you mean?"

"I mean, what exactly do you do then?"

It wasn't so much curiosity shining through this nosey question as a run-of-the-mill effort to get at the basic facts.

"Nothing at all. As you can see, I'm just a regular, thankfully well-built, guy."

"But not a nude model, right? I'm an assistant foreman at the textile factory: seventy looms and eighty girls."

"Oh, huh…"

"Exactly."

"Is Marika one of them?"

"Yeah. Well, to a certain extent," Varis stammered. "She's a seamstress."

"And you're specifically her boss?"

"Only during working hours."

"So, you supervise her at her loom, give her assignments and also bonuses?"

"And what of it?"

"Nothing at all, that's all fine."

A bitter smirk flashed across Tenisons's calculating eyes.

"What a touching scene: two perfect lovers and a rotten foreman in the middle. Taking advantage of his position. Tyrannical forced labour and material incentives… That's what you feel in your guts, right? Then you don't know Marika or her situation even a little bit."

"Probably not."

"I, of course, don't have a clue what's written in those letters. But we've decided to get married. And, in case you're interested, we're having a child. And you can be sure that if Marika didn't want it, none of it would be happening. Now think that over carefully: what kind of a girl would be writing letters to somebody else right before her own wedding?"

"I can't imagine."

"I'd actually like to see those letters."

"Why?"

"To look at the handwriting and just, well, uh… All of this needs to be sorted out. The guilty party must be found."

"The guilty party! There's no law against writing letters – everybody is allowed to do that!"

"And pretend to be someone you're not?"

Tenisons was looking him in the eyes and twisted his face as he sucked on his cigarette. "I've never forced myself on her. In our town, thank God, there's just too much of a selection for anything like that to happen. Eighty-five women for every fifteen men. According to official statistics, ages eighteen to thirty. For a girl to get married in Randava is just about the same thing as winning the lottery."

"Give Marika my congratulations. For winning the lottery."

"I'm not kidding, it's serious business. That's also why girls here try to meet men however they can: by writing letters, spending their days off in other towns. In a word, they're … nervous. The local party chairman proposed stationing a garrison in Randava. But that wouldn't work – whichever way you look at it. Almost nobody gets married during their military service and when they're done, they're off hunting birds in the bushes. Recently there's been a new idea – building an engineering plant next to the textile factory. But then there are other problems: flats, stores, schools."

"I already said – the letters are in Riga. If you like, I can mail them to you. Let's say, for your wedding."

"I just need to see the handwriting."

"That can be arranged."

"But as far as Marika is concerned, I trust her completely. I could imagine that she might have written for a while and exchanged some letters before we knew each other. I could imagine that. But why should she keep writing afterwards? Our relationship was too serious. I always try to understand the logic of every situation."

Tenisons's last words made him angry all over again. It was easy to see the confusion and suspicion hiding behind the veil of his self-satisfied boasting. This creature of logic wasn't as clever as he'd first seemed. Ignoring his strapping exterior, he appeared to have other characteristics more like those of an old man. And the fact that he was talking about love and Marika was just disgusting. Our relationship is too serious... What a twit. It was easy to imagine him dressed in striped pajamas, pacing back and forth, and stopping now and again to twist his face into a serious grimace in the mirror.

There was a long, awkward silence. Tenisons pushed his cigarette into the ashtray and stared into his eyes again like an investigator.

"So you only write poems now and again?"

"Yes."

"And you live in Riga?"

"Yes."

"I also used to live in Riga. On Dzirnavu Street by the railway bridge."

"Then we're practically neighbours."

"Did you go to school in Paegļi?"

"In Paegļi? No, at the other one."

"You wouldn't by chance know Arvīds Skudra?"

"No."

"And Vaironis Dembo?"

This was starting to feel like an interrogation.

"I don't know him."

Tenisons chortled and lit another cigarette.

"They just came to mind… Riga isn't that big. Sometimes it happens that you know the same people."

Was Tenisons saying that for any particular reason or just to make an observation? Maybe there was a threat hiding in his words?

"Well, I've woken you up and now I can go. And you're staying until Sunday night?"

"Looks like it."

"We could scoff some breakfast together."

"Thanks, but I'm not hungry."

"In that case, my apologies. I wish you a nice rest of your stay in Randava. I get the feeling we'll be seeing each other again. I'll leave you my details in case you need to reach me."

Tenisons took a small notebook from his pocket and carefully wrote down his address, then just as carefully tore the page out of the notebook.

"Today's a glorious day, I recommend walking down to the bank of the Gauja. But be careful, the Gauja is a treacherous river."

"Thanks for the advice."

Tenisons stepped back towards the door without turning around, not taking his eyes off him for the entire time, and smiling his Cheshire-cat smile. Like an armed bandit in an American Western. A total cretin. He felt like laughing out loud, but at the same time he also felt uncomfortable. This person made him angry, but somehow also something close to afraid.

He almost regretted that he'd stayed.

6

The unpleasant feeling lifted once he'd walked out of the hostel; actually it happened as soon as he'd closed the door of the "luxury suite" behind him.

He didn't end up meeting his roommate. His character and appearance could only be divined from the various items he'd left behind: a copy of *Pravda*, a scuffed patent leather suitcase, unusual foreign-made rubber boots, and a worn tarpaulin raincoat. This wasn't too different from a palaeontologist trying to reconstruct the fauna of an entire epoch from just a few fossilised dinosaur vertebrae.

The deserted hallway was reminiscent of a corridor at school in the early morning hours. Girls' voices could be heard softly purring behind the doors. Someone was singing, someone else was laughing.

The same woman who had let him in last night was still on duty. An old, plump guardian angel in a white smock. She'd put her hair up in plastic curlers and was just covering them with a kerchief.

"Did I give you back your documents last night?"

"Yes. Thank you."

"You're paid-up until tomorrow night. If you stick around here longer than that, you'll have to pay a registration fee."

"Of course."

"You got really lucky. The workers are heading home on Friday night; no one's heading back in, because everything is closed for the next two days. Of course, if there wasn't a man already waiting…"

The air was still pleasantly crisp. Cooling shadows decorated the sun-drenched spaces along the ground and across the walls of buildings. A girl was watering the planters around the Lenin monument with a hose; the green of the grass and the red of the flowers flowed together into a dazzling display of colours. The minute drops of water in the spray created a shimmering rainbow fan in the air. Steam rose from the damp asphalt as it dried.

The centre of town felt lazy and every bit like a Sunday. Families wearing bright colours, piled high with inflatable rubber swimming rings, balls, butterfly nets and all sorts of devices created specifically for the purpose of passing time, they slowly moved with dripping ice cream cones towards the riverbank. Men pushing pushchairs. Women carrying rakes and watering cans on their way to the cemetery or family garden. Collective-farm workers, in town to stock up on supplies, were milling around next to their Moskvitches and motorcycles with sidecars, along with grannies emerging in their overalls and plastic helmets, and old men with sun-darkened skin tugging at the trousers of their fashionably tailored foreign-made suits.

He kept having the urge to yawn. It would be interesting to know how many hours he'd actually slept. Five? Respectable for the most part. Though last night, of course, almost a bucket's worth of high-proof drinks had been consumed. It's a good thing his head didn't hurt. But he didn't feel like thinking. He just wanted to close his eyes and turn his face towards the sunlight. He wanted to undress, wade into the Gauja, lie on his back and let the water carry him off; he imagined himself floating along slowly, the town moving past, trees bent over the water, sandy-white shoals, blue sky.

He walked out on to the street that led across the bridge. The river shone in the morning light and resembled a sheet of polished metal. Swallows darted about, chirping. Supporting himself against the railing, he gazed into the water for so long that the river stopped moving and the bridge began to rush by.

Suddenly all of it seemed unbelievably strange: the reason he'd come here, the odd meeting at the dorm, last night's adventures. It was like some kind of nightmare. The only things constituting reality were the events of this morning and the fact that everything was flowing past him right now.

A girl on a horse. A woman with flowers. How nice that there are horses, girls and flowers in the world. He was a free person and could do what he wished…

Now, of course, he was fooling himself. He often fooled himself when he didn't want to do what had to be done. When he'd do his homework, he'd find all manner of reasons to leaf through magazines, gaze out the window and wander from one room to another. When it was time for him to wash his feet, he'd remember that he had a cold and that there was an interesting programme on television. To call someone on the phone – that was an entire problem all of its own. Guys his age considered him to be ill-mannered, because he didn't greet people he knew, he'd turn his head in the other direction and pretend he hadn't seen them. Every time he had to force himself to do anything, it summoned up an immense feeling of resistance within him.

He didn't have time for standing on bridges or losing himself in the moment. Once again he just couldn't gather up enough courage. Since he'd decided to stay after all, he should do something. At least try once more to meet Marika and the other girls. Individually would be best, one at a time. He'd been in Randava for almost twenty-four hours. And what had he found out? Nothing. He needed to go the dorm one more time, but he really didn't want to. That was much more complicated, more difficult, and more unpleasant than he wanted to imagine. And now Tenisons, who practically considered Marika his personal possession, had placed himself right in the middle of everything.

No, he couldn't go back to the dorm. But where then? Whilst trying to quickly formulate a moderately acceptable plan of action, he felt someone staring at him. Biruta, the one with the braids, was coming across the bridge directly towards him. He blushed horribly. He was dreadfully flustered, almost as if he'd been caught in the middle of some secret transgression. Fortunately, Biruta looked no less befuddled.

He stood at ease, smiled and waved. Biruta also gave him a barely perceptible wave, but turned away immediately and, keeping her head down, tried to walk past him.

"Hey, what a surprise to run into you," were the first words that came to mind and he forced them through his lips, while understanding ever more clearly that his luck had changed and he absolutely had to strike up a conversation.

Biruta didn't say anything, but looked back at him like a frightened deer. He started to walk next to her.

"It's been a while."

She smiled. Thank God.

"Where are you hurrying off to? Do you have an important appointment?"

"It's the weekend."

They were almost equal in height. Amazing. Biruta hadn't seemed that tall last night. She probably wore size forty shoes. She was swinging a shopping bag back and forth in her left hand.

"Can I help?"

"No, it's very light. Just a swimsuit."

"You're going swimming? We're heading that way, too."

"I really don't know…"

"Of course, if someone's waiting for you, if you…"

She was growing increasingly perplexed.

"No."

"So, yes, then?"

"Džuljeta promised to take me around on the motorboat…"

"Well, that's very nice. I'll walk with you."

He didn't even recognise himself and was very impressed. Fantastic! Completely the right thing to do. Now he just had to not let up.

"Have you lived in Randava long?"

"Yes."

"But exactly how long?"

"Soon it'll be two years."

"And is it fine?"

"It's alright. I'm used to it. I had a different vision for my life in high school. But then they started to push this place on us, sending us on trips to the plant, familiarising us with the course of study at the textiles institute. You know what they say about giving the devil an inch? That's exactly what happened. But… I'm not complaining."

Having recovered from her surprise, she became extremely talkative. Even excessively so, as if she were afraid that the conversation might end or slip from this innocent topic towards a different, more dangerous route.

"But four of you have to live in one room?"

"That's only for now."

"You're an optimist."

"And you're not? As far as I know… I keep thinking all the time…"

"What do you think about?"

"That… you're also an optimist."

"Maybe. Now and then."

"Your writing is that of a committed optimist."

"You've seen my handwriting?"

She shook her head so vigorously that both of her braids flew up into the air.

"No, I mean metaphorically. Your writing as a poet. Your poetry."

"Uh-huh. Yeah, yeah. Very possibly. But… well, who knows. Some critics disagree. But I don't live in Randava. And I'm not a girl."

"And what about it?"

"Somebody in the know was just telling me that Randava isn't any kind of a paradise for girls."

Biruta was confused again, but didn't turn away her gaze. "In what way?"

Did she really not understand? She's not a child.

"Well. I mean, it's boring. And just in general."

The tension retreated from her face.

"It's definitely not boring. Just the opposite: I always feel like there are too few hours in the day…"

That sounded very familiar. Marika also wrote frequently in her letters about not having enough time.

"...when you take your shoes to the cobbler, there's time to write a letter."

He stopped, took off his jacket, and threw it over his shoulder.

"It didn't used to be this hot in Latvia."

"It'll definitely rain tonight."

She leaned her head back and stared up at the sky with innocent seriousness.

"You said, 'letters'..."

"Yes, my mother lives alone in Lizums. All her children scattered every which way, to the four corners of the Earth. So, I should at least write."

She stopped again to fix her skirt.

"Do you know the address, Priežu Street 8?"

She looked surprised, but not overly so.

"No."

"I wonder where it could be? I need to meet someone there."

"It should be nearby, behind the bus station."

"Should we both walk over?"

She thought about it for only a second, no more.

"No."

"Why?"

"Just because." And, pausing for a moment, added a bit more coyly, "Džuljeta is waiting for me. I've already told you."

"Then let's leave it. There's no rush. Miss Capulet, of course, comes first."

Parts of the riverbank were gently sloping with only a narrow strip of sand separating it from the meadow. Other parts were sheer or had collapsed, and were overgrown with bushes, deciduous trees, and the occasional pine. The assembled humanity was varied, congested and undulating. Naked forms eating, drinking, laughing, chatting, occupied with transistor radios, tossing around balls, playing badminton. Blankets, towels, and sheets were laid out in amongst the white, pink, and brown shapes. Piled high on top of these – like at the market – were all manner of dishes and food. Children were splashing around in the water, crying and squealing.

"Where could she possibly have got to?"

"You can't take the motorboat any further up towards the high-voltage lines. It's too shallow."

They pushed their way carefully through the crowd, moving between outstretched legs and sun-blushed backs.

Immediately after the path, a whole battalion of girls was lying out in a row arranged like on a firing line, shoulder to shoulder, head against head and with a view of the river. Every passer-by became a moving target riddled with a volley of curious gazes.

He felt like he was a display in a shop window – or even worse: on a dissection table. Those eyes were measuring, weighing, touching, scratching, probing, flaying and tearing him apart.

Biruta fared no better. She looked completely out of her element, sometimes pretending she didn't see anybody, and sometimes responding, waving, saying hello and showing surprise, only to then immediately cast her eyes down towards the ground again, pretending to be blind and deaf.

"Ruta, Ruta, where are you running off to? Just unbelievably full of herself."

"Ruta pulls ahead. Ruta's best result this season."

"Hush! It's a pairs race…"

"Well… That doesn't matter…"

He tried to smile, but his face remained bored and indifferent. He was turning a coin around in his palm and whistling quietly to himself.

"You know a lot of people here."

"Our girls. From the weaver's shop."

"You're also a weaver?"

"Yes, for the time being."

"And what are you planning on being later?"

"Hard to say. I never try to predict the future. First I have to finish at the institute."

("Girls, look where Biruta is, I'm gonna faint!" – "And is that the poet from Kamchatka?" – "The one who said that he's a private first class?")

"Seems like they're talking about me?"

"That's what it sounds like."

"They even know my rank."

"Well, everybody knows everything here."

"Really?"

"Are you surprised?"

The boat had been pushed ashore and was resting in the sand. A standard aluminium model with an outboard motor. It appeared that there was a defect in the ignition, because the motor wouldn't start. A youth was angrily tugging at the starter cord while his rather chubby behind, which was stuffed into work trousers, was sticking straight into the air.

"Džuljeta, we're here," said Biruta.

The first surprise was immediately followed by a second one: that husky alto sounded familiar. Džuljeta turned out to be Caune.

"I found another passenger."

"What wonderful news."

Caune's rosy, round cheeks sagged. Sticking out her thick lower lip, she blew a tuft of hair off her sad furrowed brow. She had a haircut like one sees on horses – short and straight across.

"Give me a chance, I'll try to start it," he said.

"Thanks, we'll be fine."

"How many fit into a vessel like this?"

"It's not meant for public excursions."

"What's it meant for then? Fishing?"

"For saving drowning swimmers. Community service."

Caune was looking at him like he had just stolen the flowers off of her grandmother's grave. Biruta received the same disapproving, scornful and condemnatory look. Was this just her way? There was no way of making sense of it.

Biruta must have been expecting a slightly different kind of reception, because she looked confused again.

"See, the poet has stayed in Randava after all... We just happened to meet on the way. I invited him to come along for a ride. It would be interesting for him to see the Beku Cliffs."

She took the blame. Pretended to be magnanimous. Where did her sudden kindness come from?

"We weren't going for a joyride, but to study chemistry."

She said that just to Biruta.

"We'll study, but the poet will watch."

"Thank you, ladies. I have to agree: studies come first. Allow me to take my leave."

The realisation that he'd be able to leave in a moment truly made him happy.

Caune smiled triumphantly. Biruta, in her naivety, seemed to misunderstand this smile.

"You won't bother us at all, how silly. The Beku Cliffs are the most beautiful ones along the Gauja. And there's an amazing spot for swimming there. The water is as clear as glass, white sand along the bottom. But there is a whirlpool right next to it. Džuljeta dives there – ten metres down. Džuljeta, tell us yourself!"

"I'm speechless..."

"She's just shy. This place is a dream. But if you want to know anything about Džuljeta, then I can tell you that last summer she pulled the factory's champion swimmer out of that whirlpool."

"And you think she could also pull me out?"

"Definitely," Biruta chuckled. "Like it was nothing."

Džuljeta's cheeks turned pale.

"Biruta, you're unbelievable!"

"Do you think I'm not telling the truth?"

"How's that champion doing now?"

"He went to do his military service. He writes that it's alright. Get in, let's not give it another thought."

"And, Džuljeta, what are your thoughts on the matter?"

"I couldn't care less. If it seems so incredibly important to Biruta…"

"No doubt. Maybe Comrade Poet will write a poem about the Beku Cliffs some day."

"Sure… Of course… She's the compassionate one…"

Caune leaned down demonstratively and started tugging at the cord again. Thanks to her anger, this time pulling the cord worked, the motor lurched and, pushing out clouds of blue smoke, started to sputter loudly.

"Let's go!" yelled Biruta, clutching him by the hand. No time left to think. He jumped into the boat. The aluminium boat swayed precariously.

Caune looked right through him as if she were staring at an empty seat. Biruta smiled mischievously like a child who'd got away with some daring recklessness. As it picked up speed, the motor roared even louder. The front of the boat lifted ever so slightly out of the water, and the waves spreading out from its sides formed shimmering wings in the sunlight.

"Is it far?" he asked.

"What did you say?"

"Are the Beku Cliffs fa-a-ar?"

"No-o-o. Not fa-a-ar."

"Do you go there often?"

"Ye-e-es. Often."

"Just the two of you?"

"Excuse me?"

"Do Kamita and Marika go there, too?"

"Sometimes they do, sometimes they don't."

You couldn't call this kind of yelling a conversation; there was little choice but for them to settle down and keep their silence.

The left bank gradually became steeper; huge trees, their roots exposed, bent over the water. In shallower areas, the amber hues of the rough sandy shoals shone up through the clear water, mixing with the dark greenish shades of the hollows.

From a distance, the red rock formation looked like the

well-defined profile of a Native American. Three lonely spruces on the back of his neck overgrown with bushes made it look as though three feathers had been placed in the man's hair. A small peaceful bay nestled against the rocks, its gentle sandy slope slipping quickly into the imperceptible depths below.

The boat pushed up on to the shore and stopped. The motor sputtered and fell silent.

"Well, isn't it nice here?" asked Biruta.

"Yes, you could set up a tent and stay here for a while. You'd only need to bring a paternoster rig."

"I'm afraid you won't catch anything," Caune muttered without lifting her eyes. "Why waste your time?"

"Is it always possible to predict these things?"

"You bet. I speak from experience. Others have tried before."

Biruta went as red as a beetroot.

"Džuljeta, I'm begging you. You're really wrong. You don't understand anything…"

"How incredibly touching. A lot of different fishermen seem to have shown up here in Randava of late. And all of them think that here they can catch all they want using just a bare hook.

She needed to be put in her place. He had to say something to shut her up. But as usual, he couldn't come up with anything suitably cutting at the appropriate moment.

"The only thing you'll catch with a bare hook are sharks."

"I think it's better if we talk about something else. Please, OK?" Biruta did her best to insert herself into the middle of it all. She looked so unhappy, he couldn't help but feel sorry for her. Still, that wasn't the most important thing. Biruta was playing second fiddle right now. Caune had become very frank and outspoken, moving with full force into the front row; however, her anger was as incomprehensible as it was promising.

"It's possible to talk about anything, but what's the use? There are limits after all."

"I'm sorry, but what limits do you mean?"

"Shamelessness is no longer shocking these days."

"You didn't look this angry yesterday. Honestly."

"That was yesterday."

"And what could've changed today?"

"Guess. But now we have to change our clothes. You need to get out of the boat!"

"It'll just take two minutes and we'll be fine," said Biruta. "And, please, don't be angry."

"Let him be as angry as he wants," Caune shot back.

He jumped out on to the shore. A steep path wound around the rocks, along which it seemed possible to climb up to the spruces up at the top.

They both definitely know something. Definitely. You can't live together in a single room and not know. "Where we live, everyone knows everything," Biruta had said.

Removing Marika from the equation left Caune, Biruta, and Kamita.

What if Biruta was the one who wrote the letters?

The outboard motor roared back to life. Driven by a sense of foreboding, he walked back. The boat was already out in the centre of the river.

"You want to know what's changed?" Caune was yelling with her hands cupped around her mouth. "Ask Kamita tonight! She'll definitely tell you!"

That rat. She had the upper hand this time. Well, alright.

"Thanks!" he yelled back. "Say hello to your friends for me!"

At least it wasn't Caune. If nothing else, it was definitely not Caune.

7

The clip-clop of an approaching horse-drawn cart echoed off the forest road. A well-fed, shiny horse was pulling a cart piled high with birch branches. Each of the cart's wheels were covered by a tyre. The driver, a tall, sinewy man in a white shirt, had pulled the rim of his straw hat low across his forehead. Shocks of grey hair pushed out here and there from the gaps in the hat.

"Good day to you, sir!"

"Good day, good day," the driver responded as he brought his horse to a halt.

"Are you heading to Randava?"

"Where else."

"And how many kilometres to town?"

"Seven if you're walking."

"But riding?"

"Riding, of course, it's closer. Climb up and take a seat."

The driver waited until he'd lifted himself up on to the cart, then pulled at the reins.

"Walk, Ansis, walk!"

Ansis's tail snapped restlessly as he tried to drive away the gadflies. The light scent of the birch branches mixed with the sharp, acrid stench of horse sweat.

The driver, who seemed to have already forgotten about him, was humming a monotonous melody to himself and nodding his head in rhythm.

He gradually sank back into the swaying, green waves of birch branches and saw only the sky. A small cloud was floating along in the blinding bright blue above him, and resembling a single single shot into the sky from an anti-aircraft battery.

When Father put up a tent, he would usually first lay down tree branches underneath. Most often spruce needles and new willow shoots. He'd also put down cut ferns to make their night-time rest soft and fragrant. Once he woke up in the middle of the night and noticed that his father wasn't next to him in the tent. He wasn't afraid, but he was so accustomed to always having his father next to him. And suddenly he was alone. All alone at night, in the dark, in the middle of the forest. He couldn't believe it. He held his breath and listened, trying to hear his father's footsteps; outside there was only the howling of the wind. He called out, but his voice just vanished into the blackness outside, with no response.

When he received news of his father's death, the first thing that came to him was this childhood memory of his night in the forest: now he really was alone…

Nothing connected him to his mother. His mother had always lived a solitary life of which he knew little and understood even less. When his father would occasionally leave to go on business trips, he would stay with his godmother Kate in Iļģuciems. When his father returned, he'd ask, "Well, do you miss her, do you want to be with mum?" "I want to be with you," he'd answer. From time to time his mother would suddenly develop the desire to love and raise him, but that, thank God, never lasted long. Six months after his father's death, his mother remarried.

All alone. Alone. It felt grim.

Some would get visitors. Others would get packages, newspapers, letters. He would get ideological postcards from his retired schoolteacher Ms Alksne for the holidays, and his mother would occasionally send a colourful card from some place she'd just visited. *Greetings from Pyatigorsk! Look how beautiful the sun looks shining at the foot of Mt Elbrus. Listen, why aren't you home yet? A soldier living next to us already came back in the spring…*

He wouldn't have been entirely honest if he'd called his correspondence with Marika a game. These letters really did mean a lot to him. Why did he even try to deny that to himself? Was it because he was ashamed of having been far too credulous and open with her? Sure, up until the very last minute he'd completely believed that he was swapping trust for trust. Marika's letters seemed so honest, so real. The photograph played less of a role. He'd probably still have written her, even if her face had been less striking. The main thing was that Marika's words held a special kind of warmth, a kind of irresistible energy, which, right from the start, caused a kind of candour to well up within him that he'd never known before.

He was alone in his tent – at night and in the middle of the forest. But somewhere else there was another tent, a tent with a girl who'd also woken up to discover she was alone. And it seemed only natural that they would understand each other right away and wouldn't hide anything from each other. You have to be open and honest with somebody.

Of course he'd been duped. He'd been talking like a Catholic in a closed-up confessional and now he didn't even know who'd been listening to him.

And yet, not a single one of his letters had gone without an answer. Is it really possible to fake excitement and longing, happiness and hope like that? And what the hell for? Just for fun? Out of curiosity? Words, regrettably, aren't printed like paper money. Words don't have watermarks.

There's no doubt that he doesn't really understand women – that's a big minus.

"Walk, Ansis, walk!"

"He must be getting on. Nowadays horses are pretty rare. Collective farm workers don't use them either. They all use cars and tractors."

"But a horse doesn't poison the air, it doesn't pump out smoke. And what horses do leave behind, that's just goodness and nourishment. And let's say I fall out of a cart. What's the big deal? Try falling out of a speeding car."

"You don't like cars."

"You can't survive without cars nowadays. I just don't like anybody saying anything bad about horses. Walk, Ansis, walk!"

"Are you from the collective farm?"

"Forestry."

"Where are you going then – to the market, or?"

"No. There's an open-air dance at the stadium park tonight."

"Ah. Of course. The birch branches…"

"That's how it is. Cut them down in the country, and off they go to town. It's the same with people."

"But is anyone forcing them."

"Why does it have to be forced? They cut themselves down, wanting an easy life, and just keep piling themselves up into a heap. No goals, no sense. Afterwards they're surprised: no kids being born any more and the water tastes bad. When has a birch branch tied to a gate ever started growing again? Walk, Ansis, walk…"

"It sounds like you don't like the town."

"I don't like birch branches."

"You think where you're born, that's where you have to die?"

"There's not much sense in thinking about dying, but you definitely have to think about living. But what really is living? Looking ahead. Do you know who'll be left in my place here in the country when I die?"

"I really don't know."

"You see, neither do I."

"Probably someone from your family."

"Family…" the man laughed ruefully. "Family… I don't know where that family is. Here with me and the old woman, or there, in the town, at the dormitory with our daughters? Or maybe out at sea on the ship our son is sailing around on?"

"Well… You need to have people everywhere."

"Walk, Ansis! The birch branches dry out fast! Walk!"

Ansis was trotting along at a lazy pace. There were more billowy, white clouds in the sky. The road meandered between the forest and vast undulating fields of grain. Occasionally, a car would rush by. A hawk circled the forest's edge, its wings motionless.

The experience he'd gained from the brief intimacy with Vita didn't make anything clearer – instead, it'd actually made everything even hazier. It was Rolands's idea to organise the farewell dance for the army recruits at the summer house and it was Rolands who brought Vita that time. Later that evening she and Rolands got into a fight and Rolands drove off alone. But Vita stayed. She had a thick, stubby body, wide boyish shoulders, and rough knees which, when you held them in your hands, resembled large oranges.

She was lying on the couch, a wine glass in one hand, a glowing cigarette in the other, and laughed provocatively: "My little tin soldier, oh, my brave army man!"

Unsure of what else to do, he turned off the light and started kissing her. Vita's lips smelt like saliva and looked dangerously dark set against her bright face. She was wearing a thick wool dress; a sweaty warmth flowed through the fabric. He was hot too, but shaking as if he were freezing cold.

"OK," said Vita, "there's no sense lying around in these clothes, show me where the toilet is." Vita didn't come out for a long time. He tried to listen over the pounding of his heart. There was splashing water and the sound of clanging buckets. Taking advantage of the moment alone, he carefully combed his hair and checked his teeth in the mirror. She returned flushed and refreshed. She was carrying her freshly washed panties in her hand.

He was terrified and completely convinced that in a moment he'd make a complete fool of himself. He felt this way in spite of the theoretical armament he'd carefully assembled over the years, which contained the wisdom of the Song of Solomon as well as the popular scientific tracts of Forel and Van de Velde.

Still, this pitiful and confused amateur had an unhoped-for success. Practice turned out to be much simpler than theory. Simpler and at the same time utterly mysterious, because what he'd accomplished couldn't possibly be everything. Reality appeared to constrict poetry and even though for a few moments it seemed to embrace the entire world, the miracle he was expecting was overshadowed by anatomical concreteness, which his nervousness and lack of experience rendered more an act of discovery than beauty.

As morning approached and he was dozing, Vita said, "I hope at least you won't laugh about me on the inside. Which one am I? Your ninth or tenth?" And for some reason she started crying.

He felt sorry for Vita, guilty and at the same time as if he'd received an enormous gift; he put his arms around her protectively and held her. Quietly he thought to himself, You are a wonderful girl. The best one I've met. Why would I laugh about you? But out loud, he teased her mercilessly, bragged, and blurted out all sorts of nonsense, because he'd rather have had his head ripped off than admit that she'd been his first. He tortured and hurt her not out of evil intent, but out of the fear that she might sense the truth.

"No rain tonight, I think?"

"Probably not. It'll stay good for a while."

"Hot though."

"It'll be a cold winter."

"Are winter and summer really connected that way?"

"Everything's connected. How else could it be?"

"Maybe that's just in your mind."

"Have you ever seen a horse with three legs?"

"No."

"Me neither. Walk, Ansis, walk!"

They arrived in town. Music and tempting aromas of food streamed from open windows. The ice cream stands were surrounded by a mountain of empty containers. Mārtiņš had washed out the kvass barrel in the station square and it was now standing there, solitary and abandoned. The sweltering air was rising up from the baking walls and cobblestones, mixing with the scorching heat pushing downwards from the sky. But other than that nothing had changed. People walking around in their Sunday best flowed down the streets with no particular aim as cars and motorcycles drove by. Suddenly his gaze froze as though it had been shot as it leapt through the air. Kamita Kancāne was standing outside of the bread shop with the old woman from Priežu Street 8! Kamita looked at her watch, said something, the woman nodded, then they both walked off, each in their own direction.

It had happened so quickly that he hadn't even managed to sit up. His first thought, who knows why, was to hide, become invisible, and after that came the desire to watch and see what happened next but, while he was collecting himself, the cart turned down an intersecting street. There was no sense in trying to follow Kamita: she'd already invited him to meet her at 7 p.m. on the Gauja shore, at the lifeguard station.

The last thing Biruta and Caune had yelled from the boat – "Ask Kamita tonight! She'll definitely tell you!" – now took on a different meaning and tone. But if Kamita didn't show up? Her invitation might just have been a joke with the unkind aim of fooling him even more.

The clock already said three. No need to go crazy. There's still time. And this thought calmed him down a bit.

He knew after all that he'd definitely go. Somewhere deep down in his heart this realisation excited him and filled him with a renewed sense of hope as well as nervous energy, but he was happy he didn't need to go right away.

"I need to turn right," the man said, "you'll probably be getting off here."

"Yes. Thanks for the ride."

"The hostel is right here."

How did this old guy know that he needed the hostel?

"Ansis, Ansis, we've brought bad goods. The birch branches are completely crushed."

"I wonder if it was a good idea to sit on them."

"Do you think anybody will even notice? Nobody goes to a dance to look at branches."

8

His room looked like it had been cleaned up, but his neighbour's things were still sitting there untouched. Water had been poured into a carafe. He poured himself a glass and drank it down in a single gulp: it was warm and tasted of chlorine.

Yellow light the colour of beer was pressing through the thin silk curtains. He threw down his jacket and shirt and fell into bed. His joints felt heavy like after a long day of exhausting work.

He slumped across it diagonally for ten minutes, then got up and walked towards the bathroom. The showerhead had been broken off, though some kind of moisture was still dripping out of it. The sweaty pipes howled and groaned angrily. He glanced at himself in the mirror so he could comb his hair and jumped back: his black beard had sprouted all over his chin, a Neanderthal lookalike that couldn't show himself in polite company. But here in Randava, there was little hope of finding a barber's shop open on a Sunday.

His shirt collar also looked smudged and wilted, which might possibly be acceptable, but the beard had to go. He knew himself well. He had countless deficiencies already. And whenever he met girls he remembered them all: uneven teeth, a small purple splotch by the right corner of his mouth, a snub nose... If he didn't shave off his beard, then he'd just spend the whole time touching his chin and feeling like he'd committed a crime.

His neighbour's straight razor was sitting on a glass shelf next to a toothbrush. There was no honour in touching a stranger's possessions, but right now he saw no alternative. But you had to know how to shave with that kind of razor. After all, one had to run its sharp blade right up to one's throat. His neighbour was apparently a brave man, though a little conservative by nature.

He just needed to find some paper so that he could clean the shaving cream off the blade. His neighbour's newspaper was lying on the bedside table, but it would probably be wrong to tear off a piece of it. He rummaged around in the wastepaper bin which, luckily for him, had not been emptied. An empty pack of cigarettes. A torn plastic bag. A crumpled-up stack of telegrams.

"I don't know when I'll be back. Act according to your own instincts."

"I was wrong. Come right away."

"The 3 May letter never existed as far as you're concerned."

"No sense in continuing this sorry exercise in futility. Let's accept the result, which we have no power to change. We're too old to be fooling ourselves with illusions."

"I haven't forgotten anything or forgiven anything."

"Idiot. Idiot. Idiot. Hhphyuyum."

Scratches, crosses and flights of fancy. No recipient, no signature. Blank on the other side.

The operation turned out to be painful. The knife tore more than it cut. After diligent and bloodstained efforts, his chin looked as though it had been whittled like a piece of wood.

For a moment he thought someone was walking around the flat. He held his breath and listened. The wind was rattling the open window. Fool. And if his neighbour did come home, what was the big deal? Absurd.

He was sick of his tendency to be shy and too much of a rule-follower. At school he had never got into a fight, even if the other boys hurt him in some way, because fighting was against the rules. Once he gave all of his money to a drunk because he felt too ashamed to say no. He never tried to cross the street on a red light, and on the tram he'd often pay a second time if the machine didn't spit out a ticket the first time.

And what if this wasn't honesty but cowardice?

Everything was fine. His cheeks hurt, but at least he didn't feel ashamed to show his face in public. The telegrams disappeared into the toilet with a whistle so shrill it sounded like a ballistic rocket lifting off, straight into the air.

Now he could go to lunch with his mind at ease.

Just as it had been yesterday, the restaurant was gloomy and half empty. The glass doors to the balcony were half open. Where to sit? At the same table as yesterday? He didn't feel like a stranger any more. Nina had a different dress on today. It hugged her body so tightly that it revealed the form of all her underwear. And there was Gatiņš too, barely visible behind a stack of empty beer bottles and an ashtray piled high with old cigarettes and ashes.

Gatiņš got up, though that didn't make him much taller; he nodded a greeting and remained standing. Did that mean he had to go over to his table? It seemed like it.

Gatiņš looked confused and surprised, as though he'd been caught in the act. For a moment, it was hard to get any sense out of him. His glasses kept sliding down his nose and he kept pushing them back up. His brow crinkled and furrowed, he apologised, laughed uncomfortably, shrugged his shoulders, and motioned with his hands.

"...well, anyway ... you see ... well, of course..."

"Clearly. How could it be any other way?"

"Osmotic diffusion, doing crazy things with C_2H_5OH, of course, if I'm not imposing on you."

"Nonsense. I need to eat. My head was spinning like a record this morning."

"No, I'm saying this to you... as a heavily prevaricated proctophantasmist..."

"You must have been up late last night."

"Proctophantasmist. God's honest truth. Cool and clear."

"How would that be in Latvian?"

"Don't you know? Proctophantasmists have nightmares induced by constipation. Johann Wolfgang von Goethe described proctophantasmists in *Faust*."

"I never got through that little book. I tried seven times, but..."

"Too bad. Goethe is a fine poet after all. That's well known, but not in Karl Hugenberger's translations."

And while you're sitting and waiting,
From the foamy sea,
Shoots forth, moans sweetly,
A rather wet lady…

"And where's the professor?"

At that moment Ņina walked up and, glancing over rather indifferently, as if he were a coat hanging on a coat rack, handed him a menu. She was tapping a beat with her ballpoint pen against her notepad. He ordered right away.

"You and I had been introduced of course. But at times like those, the movie plays on two different tracks: the sound and image are separate. I feel guilty. I'm not making excuses. If I'd only known your last name…"

So then, Gatiņš knew. Someone had talked about him when Gatiņš was present. Maybe last night after he'd left, maybe this morning. With Aparjods? With Marika there?

"I'm afraid that you didn't miss much. Especially if you like Goethe."

"It's a question of honour. The principle of it. There aren't many decent people left in this world."

"Well, that depends on who you consider a decent person."

"Some have physical courage. But the kind of person who can rise above their own personal interests… Goethe wasn't capable of that. And Garlieb Merkel told him exactly that at a dinner in Jena with the anatomist Loder."

"Goethe was a court diplomat, a crafty aristocrat."

"It's easier to be a diplomat than a decent person. And that's exactly why those who are most respected are those who have the courage of their convictions and defend them to the end."

"And you think that I…"

"You're his son."

He felt his face flush and looked down at his watch so he wouldn't have to look Gatiņš in the eye.

"Regretfully, I only got to listen to his lectures for one year. During my first year."

"Of course."

"What happened to your father after that?"

"After what?"

"After Lysenko had dealt him the 'final blow'?"[3]

"He began to work at an experimental lab."

"That much I know. But how did he deal with it? What did he think? What did he tell you about it?"

"I don't remember. He never brought his work home."

"Even back then?"

"That was his nature. In the end he was often ill."

Ņina brought lunch. The steak cooked in fat smelt tempting, flooding his mouth with saliva. His appetite was considerable, and absorbed in the pleasure of eating a delicious meal, he let their conversation pause momentarily. Gatiņš, drawing his dishevelled head into his hunched shoulders, watched him with an understanding smile through the cracked, smudged lenses of his glasses. Suddenly he flinched, slapped his fist against his forehead, and poured some beer into his glass.

"I'm very sorry… what a terrible oversight…"

He was thinking about something, but apparently couldn't summon up the courage to talk about it and so fell silent again.

"Good, let's both have one."

The bitter brew and generous meal made him feel pleasantly drowsy.

"Aparjods mentioned yesterday that you work at the prison high school."

---

3   Trofim Lysenko was an ignoramus and a charlatan who, with Stalin's help in the field of genetics, and using draconian methods, tried to introduce his own unscientific theory of genetic inheritance in the Soviet Union (author's note).

"Exactly. Under a learning regime based on strict discipline. Does that surprise you?"

"Maybe a little. Why do they need instruction there?"

"Because they're dumb. Let's say a boy wants to play around with a girl a bit, but it turns out – that's rape. Tell me where can we talk about these things with young people openly? An indecent topic. In court. Yes, in a session behind closed doors."

"You must be an idealist."

"Let's get along without throwing insults at each other. I'm a biologist."

"And what will happen with them?"

"Many of them will turn out to be decent people. The rest will be repeat offenders – especially dangerous ones at that, as they will be somewhat educated."

"Were you selected or did you choose it yourself?"

"It would be hard for a teacher to find a better place. A better salary, firstly, because the students are difficult, though in this case without any mental deficiencies. Secondly, impeccable discipline. Thirdly, if in a normal school a student ends up going down a bad road, it's the teacher's fault. Here, on the other hand, every student who turns into a decent person is considered an achievement. Let's drink to that too!"

The beer didn't taste as good any more. He'd found that usually he only liked his first glass of beer.

He looked at his watch again. That was rude, of course, but he was a little nervous.

"I had a bit of a question," Gatiņš grimaced severely for a second and then raised his hand like a student. "Tell me, was Aparjods really as much a friend of your father's as we heard yesterday?"

"Honestly, I really don't know. It's completely possible."

"That's funny. To tell you the truth, Aparjods was acting out of character yesterday. For him to speak to someone in a restaurant…"

"I don't know. Do you consider him a decent person?"

"Aparjods?" The glass froze in Gatiņš's hand.

"So, you don't?"

"Hm. It's interesting to chat with Aparjods."

9

It seemed incredibly important to him to arrive at exactly seven o'clock. There was absolutely no way he could be late; it was always rude to keep a lady waiting. At the same time, by arriving early he'd present himself in a really disadvantageous light. By showing his interest and the weakness of his character – his impatience and anxiety. The best version of events would go like this: he walks up slowly, casually, even slightly aloof, as if he'd just been taking a stroll, but showing up at exactly the right time, glancing nonchalantly at his watch and saying, "I'm sorry, I think I'm a quarter of a second late…"

In town, where there's a stairwell at every turn perfect for hiding, a gate to slip behind, or a grocery store crowd to melt into, it wouldn't be hard for him to do this, but the lifeguard station was on the riverside, almost completely exposed. He'd incorrectly assumed that ten minutes would be enough to make his way there from the hostel. How stupid! Why didn't he just time the distance this morning? No time left for any kind of casual, slow walking; he had to bolt over there like a racehorse.

Walking out on to the path across the meadow, it was already clear to him that he'd never make it in time. Kamita might not be waiting. If he really were short on time it could still be excused, but he'd been standing around chatting with Gatiņš at the restaurant…

The "market" on the riverside had ended. Just a few groups of tipsy drinkers lying around in the grass by the forest's edge. The pine trunks were glowing pink in the light of the evening sun. The wind was chasing torn scraps of newspaper across the meadow.

He was almost running, his eyes fixed on the little white building with the yellow tower. Terrible luck. But now, stop! Things are how they are. Slowly and with a smile. Seven minutes late, there's no changing that.

Behind the lifeguard station, someone had hung a swing from the crooked birch growing there. Kamita, gripping both ropes with her hands, was moving gracefully through the air, carefree and swinging her legs, which were naked up to her hips. Biruta was standing behind her and from time to time would give her a strong push, sending the swing upward again with more force. They both looked dressed-up for the occasion and dazzling: in stockings, wearing necklaces, their hair done, faces and nails painted, their silk dresses rustling and shimmering, their shoes with a mirror-like sheen, suspended in a cloud of scent. Kamita was smiling mysteriously and seemed to be in the best of moods, while Biruta appeared to be befuddled, anxious and shy; she was fidgeting nervously, moving off to the side, and gazing off across the river.

"Well, look! But you, Biruta, said that the young man wouldn't be coming."

"Kamita!…"

"Come, come closer and give me your hand. Well-bred young gentlemen lift ladies out of their swings."

"Good evening. I completely forgot… Just awful."

"That you have to give a lady your hand and that you must be well behaved?"

"That today is your birthday."

Kamita laughed. Supporting herself on his shoulders, she jumped nimbly from the swing. And they stayed close to each other like that, looking each other in the eyes. It was a stunning moment, his legs were tired, but he couldn't give in, her challenge to him was written all too clearly across Kamita's face: she was just waiting for him to retreat, to reveal his disconcertion, to do something stupid.

"Not a problem. My birthday is cancelled."

"What do you mean – cancelled?"

He was conscious of his sweaty forehead and crooked front teeth, though he was thinking only about Kamita. It was impossible for him to find even the slightest fault in her face:

her dewy, rosy lips reminded him of freshly peeled sweet flag roots; her teeth were bright white; her skin was smooth and as iridescent as an apple peel; her eyelashes shone like thick, black rays around her large yellowish eyes.

"Incredibly simple. The executive committee changed the program. Biruta! Maybe you can finally say something coherent too."

"I have to apologise first… Sometimes Džuljeta is unpredictable. A little while ago things got a little uncomfortable…"

"You can take care of your personal business later," Kamita didn't let Biruta finish. "Let's not mix private and public matters."

Biruta had definitely told her everything. They really worked in sync.

He took a few steps in Biruta's direction, just so he could free himself from Kamita's unnerving degree of proximity.

"It was an amazing trip," he said with exaggerated indifference. Kamita's unbroken gaze provoked in him the foolish desire to brag: ultimately weren't his words irrelevant and all that mattered was the fact that he was talking? "I just can't understand what I did to have Džuljeta get so mad at me?"

"I sense that any moment now you'll also be wondering the same about me."

"Why?"

"By your inattentiveness. Aren't you even a bit interested in what happens next? The birthday party was delayed due to unforeseen circumstances. We're going to the dance."

"The dance?"

"Yes. At the stadium park. Is that an unpleasant surprise for you?"

"No, just the opposite. I've got a few acquaintances there."

"Birds?"

"No, branches. But where's Marika then? Džuljeta probably doesn't occupy herself with banal trivialities like that."

"Dance secrets, just like war secrets, aren't revealed ahead of time. So, everything's fine then? We can go."

"Džuljeta doesn't really feel that well." Biruta stared down at the ground blushing.

"Biruta! There's no time to waste."

"We'll be much too early. It never starts on time anyway."

"Let's show Sandris the park. And get some fresh air."

It was the first time someone had called him Sandris. It sounded especially nice coming from Kamita's mouth, so natural and unforced, like he couldn't possibly have any other name.

"Sounds good, let's go," he announced, "but don't hold it against me, I haven't danced in three years."

"No worries, no worries," Kamita's long black lashes fluttered like a butterfly's wings, "we know how to manage, even with the shy ones."

The stadium park was on the far side of town; past the family homes hidden behind gardens, the pavement ended and was replaced by a sandy track. Fields of grain, potatoes, and fodder beets extended out from both sides, with daisies and thistles growing in the dusty white roadside ditches. The old spruce forest came into view a bit further on. It was tall and jagged like a fortress wall. The ticket sellers were still in the process of setting up their tables past the taut ropes along the road, and were looking for the best place for them, unpacking their briefcases, counting their books of tickets.

A greyish twilight filled the space beneath the branches of the giant spruces in the park; wide and slanting as though from a film projector, beam after beam of rosy evening light streamed through the branches. A few light bulbs, which had been turned on too soon, shone bare and dull above the dance floor. The musicians had stripped off their shirts and were pulling and twisting cords on the small stage, testing the microphones, and strumming their electric guitars.

For the moment, the rows of benches around the dance floor were empty, with only a few places being taken in the first one. The girls all looked about the same age and like they all knew each other; they were sitting clutching each other's hands; stuck together, these little groups made this scene seem like a school assembly, where different classes typically form into sharply defined groups.

Some of the girls seemed familiar from the river that morning. Biruta was confused again and looking uncomfortable, but Kamita strode in, head held high, not paying any attention at all to the obvious glances she received.

"Are these girls some of yours?"

"Mainly from the factory."

"But where are their partners?"

"Don't worry, they'll have partners. Just look, some of them are already arranging themselves over there, around the bushes."

"Also from the factory?"

"From all around. From the factory, from the town and nearby collective farms."

"They look a pretty lively lot, just a bit on the short side."

"All kinds of halfwits come to these dances. A miserable bunch. The long hair and bell-bottoms are not the whole of it. They can't even grow a beard yet. But mainly, they're just unbelievable idiots."

"Does that make it hard to dance?"

"It depends on the person. All I can say is that for me it's a problem."

"The band is strong though."

"The band's good. The Randava Five. The district committee argued and debated whether the secretary of the Young Communist League was allowed to play the trumpet. In the end they decided that he could."

One side of the park ran parallel to the Gauja. The scarp was high and slanted, thick with trees and bushes, but the river wasn't directly below, there was a bright little meadow in between. From the scarp a broad view extended, revealing the zigzagging stream, sandy shoals, and the opposite bank. It was as if the dark park had opened up a brightly lit window towards the Gauja.

More and more revellers were showing up. The old park gradually filled with people like an old ship with water. No change yet on the stage. The musicians kept pulling cords, testing microphones, tuning their instruments without any sense of urgency, smoking, and chatting. The lights above the dance floor occasionally blinked out, then blinked on again.

Not far from the buffet they almost collided with Marika and Tenisons.

"So-o-o," Kamita said drawing out the vowel in way that implied significance. "Of course…"

"Yes. Why are you surprised?" Marika latched herself on to Tenisons's elbow demonstratively. "We changed our minds. It's a lovely evening. And dancing is good for your health."

"But you had to go to Riga?"

"Not me, Varis did."

Tenisons extended his hand, behaving as if they hadn't already met that morning.

"Well, poet, isn't Randava the better than Riga? And don't we have first-class girls here?"

"Yes, I can see that."

"How disgusting. Don't you feel awkward," Kamita pulled angrily at his sleeve, "walking with us, but looking at others?"

"Why others? I didn't say that."

Tenisons's question seemed idiotic to him. Just as idiotic as his answer. Biruta hung her head even lower and started to crack her knuckles.

"Yes, yes," Marika laughed in an unusual way, "it's obvious you've ended up in just the right hands."

"Do you have any objections?" Kamita cocked her head inquisitively. "But as far as our hands are concerned, it's really true, they're faultless. First-class hands…"

"Yeah, you know, they get manicures on the factory's coin," Tenisons said with a chuckle. "Perks of the trade."

Biruta looked unhappily in the direction of the stage.

"They should've started playing by now."

"They're waiting for dark. Daylight dances don't work

in Randava. That's what our guys are like. Creatures of the night."

"Tell me, Kamita, just how many years old are you going to be today?"

"Varis, dear, you're becoming dull. Every year you ask me one and the same question. Can you work it out, twenty-two already! After another twenty-two, I'll be a grandma."

"That's not guaranteed. I wonder if it'll work out that smoothly for you."

"You needn't wonder."

Everyone except for Biruta was smiling and acting as sweet as could be. He was also smiling but horribly; his concentration was failing, and the skin on his stomach and his back tingled as if it were cold.

"Usually people drink wine on their birthdays," said Tenisons. "Should we walk over to the buffet?"

Marika can't drink.

Well, that's a joke.

It's not a joke. Marika is going to have a child. (In a very calm voice, looking straight into Tenisons's eyes.)

What?! Amazing news! (General confusion.) Marika, is this true?

The first I've heard of it.

Tenisons, maybe for the sake of clarity, you could repeat what you told me at the hostel? Well, this morning when you tried to get those unfortunate letters from me…

He imagined this dialogue so clearly that in his mind's eye that he could see how the expressions of everyone there would change: how Tenisons would freeze at first and then sink, how Marika would turn pale, how Kamita would jump with curiosity. The words were already on the tip of his tongue, his throat filling with sweet and satisfying glee from having his revenge. Why didn't he say anything? Because, because… uh…

"Say what you want, Varis is one hell of an escort."

"And the only one who remembered the birthday girl."

"I heard, if my memory doesn't fail me, that the birthday was rescheduled."

"Of course we rescheduled it, but is that any reason to abandon worthy traditions?"

Kamita again stood very close to him; he looked down at her shoes, and without intending to, he also looked right down the deep-cut cleavage of her dress. His gaze snapped back again and he had a terrible start, as if he'd touched something hot. Also, something strange happened: his tongue, hands, feet and eyes were operating independently. He wasn't so naive as not to understand that Kamita's behaviour was provocative and a bit too easy-going, but that was precisely why she was such an irresistible temptation. She was bold. And she wasn't afraid to openly show her interest in him. Meanwhile, he was flapping around like a shirt in the wind and couldn't string two coherent words together. For her it must have been a sacrifice.

"Well, Sandris, what are we going to do? The troublemakers aren't letting up."

"We have to keep up those traditions."

"Then why aren't you giving me your hand? That's also a good, old tradition. Even if only to spite Marika."

"She's not looking this way."

A green light flashed across Kamita's eyelashes.

"I know what I'm talking about..."

Blabbering loudly, Tenisons was leading the way, Marika on his right arm, Biruta on his left. His small, round head jerked around in an animated fashion, and it felt as though even his shiny, grey, fur-like hair was flashing a sly smile. A disgusting tomcat through and through. He knew how to fake it so well, how to purr so pleasantly. Hypocrite. Phoney. Cheat. But the hand with its large, square fingers on Marika's shoulder was a paw capable of letting out its claws at any moment. His back was also just like a tomcat's, as was his lazy, lurching gait. He was only missing a tail, which was easy enough to imagine hiding under his long, modern coat.

Since childhood he'd sometimes imagine certain people as animals. It might have been because he watched too many cartoons. Back then Voldiņš from next door ruled over the yard as its undisputed king – he picked fights, didn't let him pass, teased him about all kinds of things. It was impossible for him to beat his tormentor, who was both taller and nastier than he was, but he imagined Voldiņš as a dog and, much to his delight and satisfaction, kept detecting new canine characteristics in him.

In school, algebra gave him all sorts of problems. Passing out workbooks to the class, his teacher Mr Pupuriņš would usually say, "My dear fellow, a person who doesn't know mathematics is intellectually handicapped." It would be extremely uncomfortable, he'd blush, hesitate, and silently repeat to himself, "But you're a turkey, but you're a turkey, a turkey, a turkey."

He was especially annoyed with a lecturer from the association charged with popularising the sciences who saw nothing but "works in progress" everywhere. This lecturer was shortish, with fuzz covering the crown of his head, a large mouth that jutted forward, an often furrowed forehead and melancholy eyes. He began to look on this man as a monkey, and would listen and think, Monkeys have bare backsides, is that a work in progress or his true nature?

A long line wound around in front of the buffet. Every so often the cashier would angrily announce, "Nossing poured. Drinks only sold in bottles."

"My dear, kind lady. Is it really impossible to pour them?"

"Pour zem yourself, don't I have enough to do? Your throat burning or vat?"

"But you'd just be pouring pure delight."

"I pour out own delight, *bud'te spokoyny.*"[4]

Drinks were being distributed quickly, but weighing sweeties, eating cookies, and cutting pieces of smoked sausage were still creating a traffic jam. Others were crowding along

4   *bud'te spokoyny*: "Keep calm" (Russian)

the side of the line with their advice; calculating possibilities, giving orders, grumbling and encouraging: don't have the Riesling, have two vermouths. Or even better: one rum and two lemonades. And sprats in oil. Hey, you up in front, don't scoop up everything, leave something for others. Stop people jumping the queue, Žanis, here's two more roubles just in case. Ilga, don't make a face, you'll get it back from us on payday.

The lucky ones at the other end of the line retreated to the more distant corners of the park with happy faces, waving around bottles and rustling paper cups.

"Where should we sit?" Marika looked around, carefully studying their surroundings.

Tenisons took off his jacket in an instant, twirling it around dramatically like a bullfighter's cape and then laying it on the ground. He couldn't ignore that example and so he tore off his own jacket and threw it on the ground awkwardly. Kamita sat down right away, stretching out her legs. Biruta, seemingly filled with uncertainty, remained standing for quite a long time before carefully lowering herself on its far edge.

"Well then," said Tenisons, "to Kamita's countless grandchildren."

"You're so obnoxious; how can you talk like that? Not happening any time soon! And that's not even a toast."

"It's the best toast. I'd even say that it's of national significance. So that our people don't die out."

"It's better to show your patriotism through your works. I've got a different idea: let's drink a 'big silent one'. Everyone can wish me what they want in silence. So, let's just drink to that."

"Not a bad idea."

Marika glanced at Kamita, then at the paper cup. For a moment it looked like she wasn't going to drink it at all. She lowered the cup, but then just fished out a mosquito from the wine, after which she drank it all in one gulp.

"Thank you, Sandris," Kamita laughed.

"For what?"

"For not wishing me anything."

"How would you know?"

"I saw where you were looking. Tenisons, didn't you see too?"

"It's important not just to see everything, but also to know what one should and should not see." Marika looked around and seemed extremely relaxed.

Biruta had only been listening half attentively the entire time and all of a sudden rose up on to her knees and gave Kamita a hug.

"Why don't you all look at the bluish grey clouds, the red sky, the dark black trees instead? Their beauty is overwhelming. It makes me want to cry. And what silence, the whole world is completely still. Almost as if at any moment, something unexpected, something unusual, were about to happen…"

And right at that moment the band started playing, the piercing sound of the speakers cutting across the entire park.

"Biruta, you're psychic, honestly!"

"You're laughing, but I'm being serious. I have this strange premonition: something will happen."

"Something's always happening."

"Maybe the skin of one of the drums will break."

"We don't know how to be honest. We think one thing and say who knows what else. And we fool each other about ourselves. You might think that this is done to deceive, but really it's out of fear, or maybe shame."

"Biruta is shaming us…"

"A very principled critique, mixed with self-criticism."

"Not at all – why do you think that right away? But this thought just shot into my mind. Would it really have been better if I didn't say it out loud?"

"Very good. Long live honesty! Down with deception! It's never too late to change. From this moment on…"

"Friends, I've got it!" Kamita pushed Biruta aside and also rose to her knees. "Let's play Honesty! I saw it in a French movie. It was extremely interesting. One person asks a question, but the rest have to answer one after another."

"And you can ask anything that comes to mind?"

"Absolutely anything. Well, should we play? Sandris! Tenisovičs!"

He didn't think about his answer, that was unimportant. He quickly tried to organise his thoughts and figure out what to do if they really played this game.

"I don't care. Heh, what's it to me…" said Tenisons.

It would be like undressing in front of everybody. Somehow that's crazy. "Fine," he said, "let's do it."

"So, let's go ahead and play? Great. Who'll ask the first question? Will you let me?"

"Thanks," said Marika, "but I won't be part of this fun little game."

"Too bad."

"I hope you'll survive without me."

"I think I probably won't play either." Biruta looked around nervously.

"How come? You're the one who's all for honesty."

"That's exactly why."

"Rechebe nu."[5]

"Kamita, if you think you can give an honest answer to any question, then you're fooling yourself."

"Why couldn't I? Of course, I can."

"Then there's no time to waste," he was like a man bent on suicide playing with a loaded revolver.

Nobody answered. This unexpected silence, following the loud and endless banter, cut through the air like a bolt of lightning: everyone was completely still for a moment and became very serious as they waited for what would happen next.

Marika got up first. As if nothing had happened, as if she was simply bored of sitting on Tenisons's jacket. Varis understood and followed her immediately.

5   *Rechebe nu*: "Say no" (Bulgarian)

"Going on like this, we might do nothing but talk until the dance is over. Jokes are jokes, and work is work. Let's go dance."

"Friends, really! There's no time to slouch around!"

"Oh, my legs fell asleep! How awful!"

Kamita was patting the wrinkles out of her clothes and stretching out her stocking seams. Looking into a small mirror, Marika applied lipstick and then wet the end of her finger and ran it across her eyebrows.

"Well, shall we go?"

The inviting sounds of the waltz had clearly aroused a degree of restlessness in the park that murmured and rustled, but this nervous activity had not yet made it to the illuminated dance floor. Groups of young men hung back behind the bushes and gradually pushed together into an ever tighter circle, as if they were planning a difficult and dangerous attack. They smoked in silence, looking around attentively; they tugged at their ties and straightened their hair, always with an air of preoccupation.

The young women sat around the sides of the dance floor looking almost paralysed, their faces appearing pale and tense in the light that shone from it.

The waltz ended. A few couples managed to breech this living wall and claim the few remaining empty seats. There were children running around in front of the stage, yelling loudly and forcefully pounding their feet. Three brave souls with sad faces studied the crowd and attracted everybody's attention as they walked awkwardly and unevenly across the raised floor several times, every so often turning to someone to ask, "Have you seen Žeņka?"

The band began to play dance music with a fast tempo and a strange rhythm.

"Well?" Kamita cooed into his ear, "I don't know about anybody else, but I want to dance."

"Nobody's dancing."

"Well, and so what? They won't be getting up to dance anytime soon."

"Back in my day, everybody danced the twist. I haven't had a chance to learn the newest hits. Is that the shake?"

"In Randava, everything that's faster than a funeral march is considered to be the shake."

"I don't know the shake."

"Then let's dance the tango. Or do the polka."

He didn't really remember how it all happened, but he found himself on the dance floor. Just the two of them, grabbed and groped by hundreds of inquisitive stares. A complete idiot. He was expecting public ridicule and yet he couldn't say no to Kamita. And better still, he felt happy. So he wasn't really a coward. He had courage. Could it be that his fear of showing his faint-heartedness to Kamita was stronger than his fear of showing everybody his inability to do the shake?

Kamita was waiting for him to take her in his arms. He extended his long arms, just barely touching her back, which was wrapped in a thin layer of silk, but she was smooth and warm and slid up so close to him that their knees bumped together. The carefree smile had vanished from Kamita's lips; she now looked quite serious, radiating an almost solemn ceremoniousness. Her body, which seemed to have grown heavier, sank down on to his elbow with an almost submissive helplessness, yet at the same time remained firm, poised to respond to even the tiniest movement.

The first steps didn't work. He wanted to pull away, but somehow it happened that he pulled Kamita even closer, so close that he could feel each beat of her heart. He couldn't breathe, his throat was dry and, to hide all of that, he tried to speak as energetically as possible.

"Well, what are we going to dance then?"

"Something exciting."

"The *pas de deux* from *Swan Lake*?"

"I don't care if it's the 'Dance of the Gladiators' from *Spartacus*."

"When I was a child I couldn't understand how ballerinas

could spin around on their toes. I thought that they must have special screws in the tips of their slippers, so that when their partners would spin them around, I thought that they would screw them into the ground."

"Lovely."

"They're looking at us as if we've just climbed out of a flying saucer."

"Do you care how others look at you?"

"Not even a little bit."

"We're not doing anything wrong after all."

"Heaven forbid."

Holding each other tightly, they were standing almost motionless, just gently swaying to the rhythm of the music. What was happening now was something resembling water-skiing. First, there was disbelief, trembling muscles, shallow breaths, and white knuckles clutching the handle connected to the line. And then all the heaviness disappeared and the water transformed into shimmering brilliance racing beneath the skis. This transformation and the realisation that "yes, I can" became the dominant emotion which couldn't be diminished even slightly by the fact that the water was still water and he was still a human being sinking into it; a completely new relationship had formed between them.

"In a minute, this place will be thick with people. They just aren't able to summon up their courage yet and take a risk, because they're always looking at everybody else and only do what everybody else is doing."

"And you never do what anybody else does?"

"No. I only do what I want to do."

"Also, dancing?"

"Also, dancing."

"Not keeping with the music?"

"Listening to the music."

"Listening, but ignoring it?"

Kamita, pretending to be angry, tore herself away from him, but soon calmed down and held on to him even tighter than before. They looked at each other, completely oblivious to everything that was happening around them. Her face was so close, he was afraid to breathe; Kamita's black pupils, constantly searching for his gaze, seemed at moments to melt together. There was no sense any more in uttering empty words. Every now and again Kamita would gently arch her eyebrows and close her eyes, bringing together her long, dark lashes; she would also smile mysteriously, her open lips curved slightly, as if she were remembering something funny and dear to her. He was filled with a strange feeling of peace mixed with quiet pride. He was proud that Kamita was so beautiful and so close to him. He was also proud that it was just the two of them dancing this sylphidine dance. Everything had suddenly changed in the world, but he'd only discovered that because he'd come here, had by coincidence ended up at this dance, and had even more coincidentally met her, someone he might never have met at all. But was it so coincidental?

"Listen, what are you two doing over there?"

Hearing Tenisons's voice was jarring. He flinched. Varis and Marika were facing each other, throwing their hands and feet around, and vigorously dancing the shake.

"You have to start with a warm-up."

"Don't fall completely asleep."

"Did you come to wake us up?"

The invisible wall was breached as a whole horde of dancers poured on to the floor. But the band decided to stop for an interval.

10

There were moans, groans and discontented murmurs; some tried to butter up the musicians with thin applause. But the song wasn't repeated and a wave of mumbles and grumbles spread here and there through the crowd. Kamita, her head held high, looked around triumphantly. An ecstatic pride was driving him along, and he felt positively dizzy with delight. The more committed ones were still applauding. *Nitwits, serves you right. So you've got long faces now? Well, there it is. Watch and be jealous…*

Kamita obediently hooked her arm around his elbow. Some couples stayed where they were as they awaited the next dance, others pushed, shoved, crowded together.

"Kamita, good evening!"

"Oh! It's you…"

"Hey, sweetheart, what's wrong with you? Come over, come over here!"

"To go for a walk, or …? You know, I'm actually busy."

"Come on, come over when you're asked! It's just five steps. A bit more into the light."

He'd seen this dishevelled head of hair, somehow resembling a dahlia, somewhere before. A rounded chest, rounded knees. A round bottom and white pants. What was her name, Lība or Līga?

"I have to apologise, I'm being called… Dear Lība, what do you want?"

"It's still too dark here, I can't really see."

"See what?"

"You don't feel it? Well, right over here…"

Without understanding what was happening, Kamita stepped back reluctantly. Lība, her eyes wide and staring piercingly into her face, kept pushing her towards the centre of the square.

"What do you mean? Be clearer, don't fool around."

"Here! Don't you feel it?"

Liba extended her index finger towards Kamita's cheek. Kamita grimaced instinctively and pulled away.

"Hold on, don't jerk around like you're on a chain."

Her hand rose even higher and in the next moment one of Kamita's black eyelashes was on Liba's palm.

"Here and glue it on better, that way you won't suck it down the wrong pipe, when all you can see are the stars in your eyes…"

He laughed, but fell silent again right away, unsettled by the lack of clarity at that moment and waiting to see what would happen next. For jokes like that a guy would punch you in the face. (He was convinced women weren't that nasty, though for a moment it did seem like Kamita was about to lunge at her.) And anyway, if there had been hostile intent in her actions, there was no way he could've stayed neutral. (What's a man supposed to do if another lady happens to attack his lady?) Then again, as he didn't completely understand local customs, he could have been expecting conflict where none was ever going to happen. And what if her eyelashes really were about to fall off and Liba's attentive eye had happened to catch it?

It seemed like Kamita was also unsure. She stood around for a while without moving. (During those minutes the dreamy elation he'd been feeling left him completely. Kamita didn't seem as enchanting any more. He didn't know why, but for some reason he felt shame and pity for Kamita.) Then her smile returned to her face. Snatching the eyelashes, she hugged Liba tightly and whispered something into her ear.

Liba's face froze like an image on a movie screen when the projector stopped.

"No," she said, "no."

"Yes, my sweet little mouse."

"Never!"

"Yes, yes!"

Liba sharply pushed away Kamita's hand and ran off.

Kamita, watching after her with undisguised contempt, looked at him and laughed: "A guinea hen…"

"What happened?"

"Nothing. When you can't yell over somebody, you have to whisper in their ear. It's good advice. A certain cashier works at our milk store, a real fury, a voice like a ship's siren. But one day I motioned to her with my finger that she step closer and give me her ear. I quietly whispered, 'My dear, I think you might be a little neurotic; don't let it take hold, that can end badly. Ask the labour union for leave and a pass to a rest home.' I only had to do it once. After that her mouth stayed closed like it had been glued shut."

"Liba and I are old acquaintances."

"Really?" curiosity flashed across Kamita's eyes. "Since when?"

"That's a secret."

"You've already met? Interesting. When would that have been? This morning?"

He shook his head and laughed.

"When? Last night?" Kamita wouldn't give up. "Don't deny yourself. It's only your second day here. Did she invite you to the dance?"

"No. We got past the lock of one of the doors together. And after that we went for a little walk across the rooftops, jumping from balcony to balcony."

"And that's all?"

"What, isn't that enough?"

"You can expect more from Liba."

"It seems to me that you don't like her very much."

"Do you?"

"She's got a pretty unique style."

"I'll say, no thanks to being too unique. The thief girl in the Andersen story also had a pretty unique style. Liba, of course, doesn't shoot, she prefers colder weapons."

"This young girl?"

"What and you didn't know that already? But you're

supposed to be old acquaintances... She's been in prison. She tried to kill someone, you know! And her little lad, well, he almost croaked! And she doesn't care about her child either. Grandma is raising it in Viļāni or Varakļāni."

"A child too..."

"Well, yeah. Children aren't so shocking, it's the mother that's a shock. But now you're free. You two can go have a smoke together." Kamita opened her hand that held her fake lashes. "Unfortunately, I have to leave your delightful company for just a bit."

"Can't I help?"

"What do you think? Magic requires solitude."

"Solitude is a boring business."

"No problem, I'll leave you a substitute. Biruta! Make sure that the poet doesn't wither away from the sorrows of the world. But at the same time, of course, keep him out of mischief! Do you hear me?!"

Kamita shook her finger threateningly and melted into the crowd. Biruta, her head hung low, moved closer.

A new dance began.

"I hope you can also keep an eye on me while you're dancing?"

Biruta blushed, but still wasn't able to conceal her happy smile.

"I don't dance that well."

Her obvious insecurity pleasantly relaxed him.

"Me neither. But this isn't a competition."

Biruta wasn't lying. Pushing and pulling her around was hard work. It seemed like all she was thinking about the whole time was how to keep a respectful distance between them. Her movements were wooden and lifeless, and she kept looking at her own feet, as she tried to calculate every move ahead of time in her mind. She tried too hard and struggled, became anxious and confused, took it to heart, suffered because of it, and trembled.

"Kamita and I were just talking about Lība. It turns out she's a noteworthy person."

"I'm surprised Lība came tonight. She usually doesn't go to dances."

"And you?"

"Me neither."

"If it's not a secret, why not?"

Biruta looked into his eyes for the first time.

"Do you know what an auction is?"

"For the most part."

"Dances remind me of auctions."

"And what of it?"

"I guess I'm not brave enough."

"Lība can't complain about not being brave enough."

"Don't laugh. I'm sorry for her."

"Sorry?"

"She's not terribly happy. I'm sorry, I really don't know how to dance. Maybe let's stop?"

"No, I'm already doing much better."

He couldn't let go of her no matter what. Ignoring the heavy stream of self-criticism that Biruta subjected herself to, she did like to dance, and their combined efforts were gradually bringing them closer: Biruta was becoming increasingly secure and talkative. Of course, she kept hiding herself behind seven different veils, but as they continued to dance, he was hopeful that just like Salome, she might toss off at least a few of them.

"I'd like to talk to you."

"About Lība?"

"No, just in general. But with complete honesty. A little while ago we wanted to 'play honesty', but I mean it seriously."

Biruta's gaze froze. She was nervous and forgot to follow her feet; she suddenly seemed to become his shadow, losing her balance for a moment.

"The girls don't know how to dance, do they? Or, more correctly, the dancing isn't the main thing. They're coming to meet guys. I mean, you can understand that, it is pretty important."

She laughed quietly, but then right away became serious again.

"But there are some who do come just to dance. I would too, if I only knew how. Dancing is nice."

"I'm incredibly pushy, but please consider it to be just due to professional interest: haven't you ever wanted to meet somebody?"

"How can I put it... I really don't know."

"Well, even if just out of pride. Or, let's say, to spite the other girls. Or just statistics being what they are..."

"I think that statistics don't mean anything. I believe in luck. A hundred lottery tickets might be losers, but just one and only one a winner."

"So you believe in destiny."

"It doesn't matter. I believe that those who have to meet each other, have been moving towards that since birth – little by little, step by step, as if they were wandering through a complicated labyrinth."

"But if this other half doesn't even exist? I mean, if they just don't mathematically..."

"They're out there somewhere. Maybe very far away, on the other side of the world, but they're there. And suddenly their paths take an unexpected turn and they meet. Just for a single moment, somewhere in the dark of the night, in the crush of people at the station, or in a crowded airport. And they understand that they've been looking for each other. Isn't that how it happens?"

Clearly, he was expecting "something" from this conversation. And for that reason he was as careful and attentive as a person connecting electrical wires without knowing what he would be turning on. Still, the result was extremely surprising. In the blink of an eye, blushing Biruta transformed into a fearless and passionate evangelist, deeply convinced of the truth of her words, ready to struggle and to fight. She was unrecognisable. Her words flowed without stopping – quickly and full of determination; her face looked almost fanatical in its seriousness, with an expression that was so wistful and elated that it made him stop in utter shock.

"Isn't that how it happens?" she repeated.

"Sometimes it does happen like that. But mostly in movies and books, I think."

"Not at all! What happens in life is beyond anyone's imagination!"

A story about a classmate and her strange destiny came flooding out of her.

But he didn't hear a single word of her story, he could only think of one thing: what if she wrote all those letters...

Was it impossible? In truth, there were many notes ringing throughout her passionately romantic enthusiasm which seemed familiar. Of course, he had no exact proof, no point of reference or fact for the moment, but if you judged her according to her style, her expressions and line of thought, then Biruta, without a doubt, was the easiest of all to imagine as the letter writer. Some qualities matched exactly: the slightly sentimental way in which Biruta talked about other people (even Lība), her sudden passion, her timid tone in speaking about herself. One part of the letters had been just about the beauty of nature, and wasn't it Biruta who suggested the trip to the Beku Cliffs and just now, while drinking wine, didn't forget to sing the praises of the sky and clouds? The friendly underlying tone in the letters completely echoed Biruta's sensitivity and shyness. And if you also took into account the trusting candour with which she spoke about her own inadequacies...

Why couldn't it be Biruta? Though this conclusion also immediately made him feel somewhat disappointed and bitter.

Of course, it was nothing but a guess. Also, Biruta is enrolled in the correspondence college, but there's not a single word in her letters about her studies. One thing was certain: he had to see Biruta's handwriting.

"I'm very sorry for you," she said. "I don't understand how someone can be a poet, but not believe in miracles."

"It's not that simple."

"I'd imagined you a little differently."

"In what way, for example?"

"You take a very romantic approach in your poetry."

"That's quite possible. You see, poets, just like schizophrenics, have split personalities. It's as if there were two different people living inside of each of them. The romantic writes the poems while the realist is asleep."

"You're joking again."

"I'm being completely serious. I'm not joking. And I have some serious news for you – you write poems, too."

Biruta turned dark red.

"Who told you?"

"Do you have any with you?"

"A poem? No… I don't."

"Too bad. I'd like to look at them."

"You think it would be worth it?"

"Definitely."

"But I've written them only for myself."

"We can make a secret compact with the motto, Not a word to anybody…"

"I'll give it some more thought."

Confidence and trust were fighting a battle with fear inside Biruta. She looked so surprised, as if she'd just woken up and was still trying to understand which of the words she'd heard belonged to her dreams and which to waking life. This sudden burst of thoughts clouded her face with suspicion-filled seriousness, but her lips were opened and illuminated by her smile like a dark cloud by the golden gossamer of the sun. The brightness of her enthusiasm and joy was already pressing through her befuddlement.

The compact, it seemed, had been made.

11

They didn't say anything to each other after that, and tried to stay quiet for the rest of the dance, though without their initial haste and palpable distraction. They mixed up their steps worse than before, their movements were hopelessly incorrect, but they didn't pay much attention to that any longer, as they were both occupied with other thoughts.

He accompanied Biruta to the edge of the dance floor, from where one could see Marika's blue dress and Tenisons's bright red tie flashing through the crowd. Biruta hurried ahead of him, but now and again she'd look back and smile dreamily like the Mona Lisa.

The sad trio looking for Žeņka appeared on the dance floor once again.

"How are you doing?" Tenisons asked Biruta.

"Well, thank you."

"Not us," said Marika, "there's no place to escape from all these mosquitoes. They're eating us alive. I was saying to Varis that a bright white neck is like the Alexandrian Lighthouse to these insects."

"But where's Kamita?" Tenisons seemed not to have heard Marika's comment.

"She's playing hide-and-seek."

"Kamita, yoo-hoo. Where are you?"

He looked around, and a short distance away noticed Lība standing in the eerie light. She was standing alone with her back against a pole and was fixing a broken cigarette. Even though she seemed completely focused on what she was doing, Lība noticed his gaze right away, shot back a cool glance, and then disappeared somewhere.

After that he caught sight of her on the far end of the dance floor, a bit further on, this time leaning against a tree. Their gazes met again, with Lība seeming even more unpleasantly disturbed, but this time she allowed herself an innocent, playful little smirk (to pretend not to see him would likely have been even more foolish.)

She disappeared again. Now it had become a joke between them. He was using all of his attention to try to find her, and wanted to catch sight of her at any cost. It was a little, quiet, absurd struggle and he didn't want to end up on the losing side.

Tenisons went to dance with Marika. Not far away, Biruta looked like a grenadier standing guard in a gown; she avoided looking in his direction, clearly out of sensitivity, so he wouldn't feel that he had to ask her to dance again. The rhythm of the music was prodding at him and making him acutely nervous; something had slipped by like dust in the wind, he'd missed it and now it was irretrievably lost. If only Kamita would come back. After so much hesitation, it would be rude to ask Biruta. And so he kept hesitating, not sure what he was waiting for or even what he really wanted.

Lïba was skulking around along the other side of the hedge, apparently thinking that no one could see her in the shadow of the stage. She could just as well have been hiding behind her hands. It would be a great trick to sneak up on her on this side and suddenly stand right in front of her:

Would you do me the honour?

No thank you, I don't dance.

We're playing a game and I found you. Let's dance.

He felt an irresistible urge to toy with surprised, confused, capricious Lïba just a little bit; it was the same rotten impulse that makes children twist and tug kittens around or squeeze weak birds in their hands. But after all, why shouldn't he play this trick on her?

Lïba had spent time in jail – that was particularly interesting. She had a child – but what of it? Just for fun. She'd be speechless. She'd be completely floored.

And anyway, there wasn't anything especially indigestible there; aside from Marika, Kamita, and Biruta, Lïba was the only girl he knew in that place (a strong statement!). Well, knew a bit. Either Biruta or Lïba... Two dances in a row with Biruta – thanks but no thanks. With Lība! It was a sure thing. Without any conditions. Just a momentary whim. A little thrill. As Aleksandrs Draiska would say, "Be ready to do anything just to feel free inside – even wiggle your ears."

But as he moved closer to Lība, his nimble steps grew slower. It wasn't as simple as it first seemed; prison and her child didn't make it any easier. Still, he had to go up to her, talk, say something. "Lightly and quickly with women like this." Not a chance. He could expect anything from this lady.

Lība had already noticed him. Now he trotted along, tied to her gaze like a fox terrier on a leash. She looked at him as she would a manifest buffoon. No hint at all of her confused, searching, stingingly ironic stare.

There was still one way out – to walk past Lība and ask one of the other girls to dance. No matter who else, just not Lība. That would be a real gag. A haughty smirk, an indifferent look over his shoulder: *Oh, Lība, you're here too, how's it going, how's it going?*

Too late. No way out now. A small, weak grin twisted by despair; gulping, unsteady breaths as if he had just jumped awkwardly from a diving board and belly-flopped into the water.

"May I ask you to dance?"

"I don't know, it's not against the law."

"What am I supposed to make of that?"

"Who can say, maybe you're afraid?"

"Afraid, ha… Why? Of what?"

"I think of Žeņka. Don't you know Žeņka?"

"We haven't been introduced."

"Just remember that I've warned you. After all, you're the one who'll have to fight, not me."

Another new fact. But, thank God, at least it wasn't a rejection. And she behaved almost politely. The easy motion with which she placed her hand in his had its own pleasantness to it.

"Honestly, I don't understand a thing."

"Very simple, he's drunk and doesn't want anybody else to dance with me."

"What's he to you, your husband or stepfather?"

"Let's just assume that that can't be revealed."

"Why doesn't he ask you to dance himself?"

"Žeņka doesn't waste his time on details."

She said that with the most innocent of expressions, as if she were reading a poem by the Christmas tree in her kindergarten class. Amazing. He apparently had no conception of this little girl's life experience. She, without a doubt, came from a completely different world with its own morality and standards – ones which were foreign and incomprehensible to him.

"I think we'll talk and everything will be fine."

"If Žeņka liked talking, he'd be working at the cemetery as a funeral director giving eulogies."

"You're scaring me terribly. Before bedtime… So, Žeņka doesn't work as a funeral director then?"

"No, he makes work for the funeral directors."

"Just for fun?"

"Nothing like that. He gets paid."

"A professional bandit?"

"Oh, what are you talking about! He works at the funeral home as a cashier and receives applications. Here we call it social services."

The chances of him having to grapple with the jealous cashier seemed fairly real. Also, while he could accept the fact that Lība was warning him, the whole depressing prediction no longer sounded as serious. But maybe Lība was just making fun of him? Somehow he didn't want to believe that. Her tone sounded almost friendly.

"In other words, I can also hope to be buried right here?"

"I doubt it."

"Too bad. It's a lovely place. Remember, there's a song called 'I Want to Die on the Shores of the Gauja'."

"Our hospital is also in a lovely place."

"And visitors are allowed in three days a week?"

"Every day for visiting the badly injured."

"Will it be convenient for you to visit me that often…"

"As far as I'm concerned, sir, you can go right back to Riga and sell your bones to the anatomical theatre."

That she called him "sir" probably meant he'd been relegated to some lower class. He had to try to make Lība smile, otherwise he really would feel like a creep.

"Thank you. Should your friendly advice also be considered part of social services?"

"If you like. Advice is advice."

"But then I owe you something. Social services are usually not given away for free." (Oh Lord, what was he going on about now… About money! A complete mental blank!).

"Well, let's just let it go this time. I didn't bring my receipt book with me. And you won't listen anyway."

"Do you know that for certain?"

"For certain. You have a cleft in your chin. That's a sign of obstinacy. My late mother, Jūla Marcinkēviča, a gypsy from Čiekurkalns, was the best fortune teller in the region."

"Then you're the blondest gypsy in Latvia."

"In addition to all of your bad qualities, you have one which is especially bad: you're sloppy. I'm not a blonde, I'm a brunette. Because my father was German, he was supposed to shoot my mother, but instead he escaped with her into the forest."

"Almost like in *Carmen*."

"Yes, and after that he himself was shot…"

If Lība was a gypsy, then he was a Crimean Tatar. Although, her eyes were actually quite dark – and as large as plums.

"Do you know how to tell fortunes?"

"I don't tell fortunes, I just see. Or I also sense things. It's impossible to describe it in words."

"Well, and what do you sense? Let's say, about me?"

Lība laughed and began humming the dance melody, to delay her answer it seemed. Careful studied attention was just barely perceivable in her flighty glance.

"It's not going well for you. You're being cheated…"

So she heard everything last night.

"Who's cheating me?"

"If you want to know, you'll find out."

"Interesting. When?"

"Soon. Today, tomorrow… I don't know."

"And what, in your opinion, should I do?"

Lība's humming grew louder, she danced with abandon, and took the lead ever more persistently, spinning him in circles on purpose.

"Do as you like. I'd leave. I don't like to be cheated. But maybe you do?"

Maybe Lība did have gypsy roots. She knew how to charm you into talking. It wouldn't take much for him to unburden himself and tell her everything. Like a dumb farm animal.

"Žeņka isn't coming after all…"

"Of course. He won't come here. It's too late and there are police everywhere."

"I'd like to get to know him. Just in case."

"Nobody has formally introduced us to each other either."

"A tiny formality. My name is Jānis Krūmiņš, I've come to Randava for work. As the platoon commander for the local division of the *milicija*."[6]

With an agonising squeal from the saxophone, the foxtrot gave up the ghost. Lība slapped her palm across her red silk dress as if she were wiping off dust.

"Not true," she said. "You are Aleksandrs Draiska. Also part gypsy. A poet or a gypsy, there isn't much difference. But Gypsies are better at lying."

He walked Lība to the hedge and with obstinate stubbornness remained standing there, blabbering on and saying any fool thing that came into his head. Lība occasionally would answer with a single word, but would look around nervously

---

6   The *milicija* was the name used for the civilian police in Latvia during the Soviet years. This was also the case in the other parts of the Soviet Union at the time.

and was clearly feeling anxious. His mood lifted though when he saw Kamita returning to the far end of the dance floor.

"I'm so sorry, but now I have to go. I hope we'll have a chance to meet again," he said.

"Go ahead then, you're not tied up. It'll be better for both of us."

Kamita received him with a radiant smile, but tried to pretend that she was offended.

"Uh-huh, I see how it is, very nice, very nice. Where were you then?"

"Occupied with dancing duties."

"With Lība, right?"

"Right, with Lība."

"And what about her – was she euphoric?"

"I'd say that the conversation took place in the spirit of unanimity and mutual understanding."

"What did you mutually understand?"

"The fact that nothing can be understood."

Kamita slid back into his arms and they embraced even more tightly than before – as if from the joy of seeing each other again. Except now it was no longer a novelty, but a return to something known and familiar. Much more pleasant, at any rate, than Biruta's wooden shyness and Lība's capriciousness. And he felt much more secure, his knees weren't shaking any more, he wasn't short of breath. Kamita's moves were balanced, there couldn't be a better dance partner. It seemed like their feet didn't touch the ground; suspended by the tempo of the melody, they twirled in the air like acrobats, surrounded by a blur of countless faces and forms.

All of a sudden Kamita stopped and, making all manner of faces, brushed both of her hands across her eyes.

"That kind of chemistry might be the end of us all!"

"Another accident?"

"Not an accident, but a mess."

"I don't dare offer you my handkerchief, it was still clean the morning before last."

"No worries, it'll be fine."

Poor thing! She must have applied too much glue when she was attaching her false eyelashes, and it was now soaking into her actual eyelashes. She could only open her eyes with difficulty. Every time she blinked, her eyelashes would stick together again.

"Let's go sit down. Should I look for some water?"

"No firemen needed! Let's just keep dancing, it'll be fine."

"Then at least cry, please."

"Let's walk down to the Gauja. Give me your hand."

After the brightly lit dance floor, the park seemed pitch-black. At first he could only make his way forward by touch, worried every moment that he might walk right into something. Gradually his eyes became sufficiently accustomed to the dark for him to see the outlines of tree branches and bushes. Lingonberry bushes scratched at their ankles, they stumbled over holes and clods of earth, their faces were unexpectedly brushed by sharp branches.

"Dark as hell."

"I don't care, I can't open my eyes anyway."

"And if I lead us to the wrong place?"

"Just try it, Sandris!"

For a split second he really did want to lead Kamita straight into a tree. But the situation did seem rather serious.

"I don't even know where we'll end up."

"Wait a second, let me take off my stockings. Though on the other hand, eh, let them tear. The ones with seams aren't in fashion any more."

"Go ahead and take them off. There's no sense wasting things for no reason."

"You're touchingly frugal. Fine, I'll take them off, just for you."

Supporting herself on his shoulder, Kamita crouched down. Her bare ankles flashed for a second.

"Well, support me, don't you have any strength at all? No, not just by holding my hand."

A sweet smell was coming from somewhere. It was sharp and intoxicating, as from poisonous flowers. Too strong, nauseating, he felt spasms in his throat and weakness in his knees. Luckily, it was dark. Fear transformed his gentle, considerate grasp into a wild, savage grip. He was expecting her to scream from pain, but instead Kamita nearly choked from laughing. She remained crouched over, working on her legs. What would happen if I lifted her up and kissed her? It's so dark. And she said herself that I should hold her.

Kamita's waist was narrow, he could almost grasp it all the way around with both of his hands. Her stomach moved gently as she laughed. To lift her up, to straighten her pale neck with her pale ear showing above it, her neck which smelt so awfully of lilies of the valley.

"But now, let's run!" He grabbed her by the hand.

He didn't want to run anywhere. He felt like he'd turned to stone. But he had to do something. He no longer doubted that he could kiss Kamita. But that was still ahead. Now he knew for certain that sooner or later it would happen, and this inevitability confused him even more than his doubts had confused him earlier.

It was much lighter in the clearing. An occasional star twinkled in the pale blue sky. The waters of the Gauja, quietly murmuring along the overgrown shoreline, swirled and shimmered. Kamita ran across the meadow, her shoes swinging from her free hand.

"Give me your shoes."

"Not a chance in the world!"

"Then I'll take them myself."

"But I won't let you have them."

He embraced her and pulled her close to him. Kamita, bending her head back, twisted side to side; in bare feet, she came up just barely to his chin. They were both out of breath, loudly gulping air. Her thick hair had fallen on her face while she was running; with a light, quick motion he pushed it back behind her white neck that smelt of poisonous flowers.

"Sandris, I can't see…"

He let her go, but that was a mistake; she laughed mischievously and ran off across the meadow towards the riverside.

By the time he reached the river, she'd already waded into the stream. The water she had scooped up with both hands broke the stillness of the night as it spilled noisily back into the river. The echoes of the music streaming from the direction of the park sounded like otherworldly voices. The campfires of fishermen glowed a pinkish red on the Gauja's opposite shore.

A numbing harmony developed between the calm that surrounded him and the tormenting premonitions that were winding him up like a spring. Now he couldn't stop, no matter what. Now he had to do something crazy, something reckless. He grabbed a large rock and threw it sideways into the river, aiming it so that the splash would hit Kamita.

She screamed and wrenched to the side, then scooped some water in her hands and went after him. He tried to hide behind a pine tree that had fallen into the river, but lost his balance and suddenly found himself in the water. And only afterwards did he hear the hollow sound of the impact, as if a sack had tumbled into the river. The water was warm and smelt of sweet flag. He was choking, laughing and spluttering as he swam around the strong current towards the shore.

"Well, see! That's your punishment! What are we going to do now?"

"Are there crayfish here? We could catch crayfish."

"In a moment your teeth will be chattering so much, it'll be a terrible thing to hear."

"The water's like a warm bath."

"Get out, wring out your clothes, and snap some dry branches, I have matches in my purse."

While he was lighting the fire, Kamita disappeared. Just as he was starting to worry and reassure himself that his suspicions of abandonment were ridiculous, she returned with a bottle of rum. The timing was perfect because he really was starting to shiver. His damp skin and wet trousers attracted the cold. The fire was producing more smoke than flames.

"No glasses, so we'll have to drink from the bottle." Kamita ran her warm palm across his back. "Brrr. You feel like a corpse. Get closer, I'll warm you up."

"You'll get an award for saving a drowning man."

"But you – whooping cough. Did you wring out your clothes? Just don't put them too close to the fire or they'll start smouldering."

"I'm sure they'll dry out."

"Drink."

"A brilliant idea. As Aleksandrs Draiska would say, 'My hat off to you and you – and also my gloves and jacket – for thinking of that.'"

The dark bottle glimmered invitingly in Kamita's hands against the light of the campfire. Warmth flowed into his veins. Flames finally shot out of the fire, along with an entire swarm of bright sparks.

Kamita's palms touched his chest.

He gripped her by her pale neck, pulled her closer, and kissed her, awkwardly searching for her mouth with his lips at first, but then with increasing enthusiasm and courage pressing so close that their teeth pushed together and Kamita became almost lifelessly heavy in his arms.

Finally she cried out and pulled away.

"You don't like mouth-to-mouth? That's how you save a drowning person." He tried to stay calm.

She laughed whilst stroking his chest.

"Oh Lord, what a dummy you are. You almost poured out…"

He was still holding the bottle in his left hand.

"Ah. There's still some in there? How nice!"

They laughed and kissed, and their lips tasted like rum.

12

Someone next to him was breathing evenly and quietly, pressing their cheek against his shoulder; his arm had gone to sleep and was smarting with pins and needles; he tried to turn on to his other side, but the bed was narrow and something heavy was pressing down on him, making him feel like he was covered with earth. The sound of the breathing stopped, but he could still feel rhythmic, warm exhalations against his cheek. He was sleeping uncomfortably entwined with another body. It was as if they had been fighting or thrown into the air by an explosion.

Finally, as he woke up completely, he began to remember what had happened. It made him want to jump up right away, because he felt like at any moment someone could come in and find him there or, if the door was locked, start knocking and create a commotion. The superintendent or one of the girls.

He moved abruptly towards the wall while trying to free the arm that had gone to sleep, but stopped almost immediately – Kamita was sleeping soundly. The sheet with which they had covered themselves was crumpled and twisted. It covered nothing, folding around them like drapery in a classical painting. A whitish strip stretched across Kamita's brown back, and her breasts also looked strangely pale, almost translucent, with small blue veins visible under her milky white skin; these gentle protrusions with reddish amber pupils at each tip held one's gaze: this was the first time in his life he'd seen a woman's naked breasts so close and so clearly. There were small holes in her ears, she must at times wear earrings.

His gaze didn't leave Kamita. At the same time, the nervous, uncomfortable feeling, as if he'd stolen something, didn't leave him either.

He remembered his suit. Kamita's dress hung from the

chair along with various other articles of clothing, but there was no sign of his suit. His shoes and socks were on the floor.

After they'd emptied the rum bottle he'd wanted to return to the dance floor, but Kamita had said he couldn't show himself in public looking how he did. They'd kept close to the shore and walked across meadows until they found an old barn.

He'd walked her to the dormitory. And then Kamita had told him not to be silly and come inside.

"You can't go back to the hostel with a suit like that."

"I'm not going to come inside, that'll mean trouble for you, it's late."

He'd kissed Kamita. Now he could. Now that wasn't hard anymore. He'd wanted to keep kissing Kamita without stopping.

"Don't be so wild. My lips hurt," she'd said. "Come on, before Maṇa goes to sleep."

"You're enough for me, I don't need Maṇa."

"We need Maṇa for your suit."

"But what if the girls show up?"

"Marika won't be here tonight."

"But Biruta and Caune?"

"Your suit will be fine again in half an hour."

He'd known which room to go to. But this time, for some reason, it seemed smaller and the ceiling seemed lower. The night light had an orange cover, Kamita had drawn the shades in front of the window. He'd removed his suit and Kamita had carried it off somewhere.

Kamita's face was plastered like a playbill across large parts of his memory: when they'd returned to her room, she'd stood next to him and gazed into his eyes for a long time. She may have been asking him something and waiting for his answer, but he hadn't said anything, because he couldn't hear anything. It had been as if they'd been caught in a storm; there'd been a roar in his ears and a pulsing, pounding rhythm, terribly loud and getting louder. He'd wanted to step back, but bumped into the wall; he'd lost control over his own body.

He also remembered her face in the moonlight on a white pillow – inscrutable and distant even when there was no distance separating them; sometimes her lips would curl as if from pain, but then a moment later they'd burn him with delight. He couldn't understand why her lips moved as they did, and still less did he understand the delight they brought him.

"I don't like the name Sandris," she'd said. "Many other women have called you that, I'm going to call you something else. Think of a name for me to call you."

"Maybe Kaspars?" she suggested.

"You can call me anything you like – even Kaspars."

Still, the most important thing was what she'd said in the old barn on the riverside.

"And you really didn't know it was me?"

Her voice had been tinged with disbelief and a hint of reproach.

"Honestly, I had no idea."

He saw Kamita on the corner again talking with the woman from Priežu Street 8 and heard Džuljeta Caune's voice: "Ask Kamita tonight! She'll definitely tell you!" The solution was simple and natural.

"Well, when you first came to town, little did you know that you were actually coming to see me."

"You really could've told me that yesterday. I almost went back to Riga."

"I knew you wouldn't go anywhere."

"If there'd been a train, I'd have left. Why didn't you say anything?"

"I don't know. Can everything be explained? I wanted to see what you'd do next."

"And now it's all clear?"

"Yes."

"Why?"

111

"Guess…"

Someone knocked on the outer door and, without waiting for a response, started to twist the handle. Just as he'd expected.

He jumped up into a seated position, pulling the sheet higher.

Finally, Kamita opened her eyes too, but stayed motionless.

"Someone wants to get in."

"Let them. I'm tired. What time is it?"

"Half past seven."

Kamita, stretching her arm, sighed heavily.

Right at that moment there was another knock on the outer door.

"I guess we have to get up after all. That'll be Maṇa with your suit."

She climbed out of bed and spent a fairly long time looking for her slippers. She then ran into the front hall. She'd put on her dress, but it looked sloppy and dishevelled.

"Who's there?"

No answer.

"Come back later. Sandris is still here with me."

There was no denying that, but Kamita's answer still shocked him. He was expecting her to lie. What unbelievable courage.

He heard Kamita go into the bathroom and the pipes begin to sputter. He was terribly thirsty. There was a carafe on the table. He got out of bed and drank one glass, then another. As he was drinking he also gargled and rinsed his teeth. Then he crawled back into bed.

When Kamita returned, that sweet smell wafted over him again.

"We could've stayed in bed, that wasn't Maṇa, it was Biruta."

"Biruta? Maybe she needs to get in?"

"Nonsense. Let her go over to Liba's. Liba's room is half-empty."

"And what about Caune and Marika? Look how it all turned out."

"Don't worry, don't worry."

"I could sense what they'd have been thinking when they couldn't get in here last night. Did they knock? I didn't hear them somehow."

"We weren't really listening."

Kamita came up to the bed and ran her fingers through his hair; her smile and half-closed eyes reminded him of it all.

He clasped her hand and pulled her closer. Kamita sat down on the side of the bed.

"Come over here," he said, "I want to talk. We haven't even had a chance to talk. We only know each other from those letters."

"What else do you want to know?"

"Everything."

She laughed and drove her fingers deeper into his hair.

"You're such a cad. There's no time for talking. Well fine, but just for five minutes. Move over to the side a bit more."

She took off her dress and slid underneath the sheets, pressing her warm body tightly against his. For a moment they both lay there without saying anything.

"Well, why aren't you talking?"

He probably wasn't even breathing.

"Well, fine then, just as I thought…"

Kamita's fingers scratched at his neck with their sharp nails. She laughed and nibbled at him. And after he pressed her mouth shut, she kept laughing with her eyes. Then, when she closed her eyes, she kept laughing with her breath. And it seemed to him like her laughter rose up to meet him and he sank into it; her laughter became quieter and quieter, rippling somewhere high above him like a trembling gust of wind blowing over calm, open waters.

This time he woke up after her. Kamita was already up and dressed. A kettle was whistling in the kitchen.

"It looks like you're the sounder sleeper, it's almost ten o'clock. Now it's definitely time for you to get up."

"Your proposal is received with thunderous applause. I just don't see my suit anywhere."

"Go and get washed up first. Meanwhile, I'll go and see Mana. You can use the pink towel, it's clean."

His head hurt a bit. He bent over the bathtub; the shiny fixtures momentarily fogged over as he observed them. He stepped into the bathtub and used the showerhead to rinse himself, his mind growing noticeably clearer from the brisk spray of water. As he dried himself off with the rough towel, his skin stung as though it had been burned.

A genuine ladies' paradise: freshly washed shirts and stockings, all sorts of little boxes, bottles, and containers.

His hair was messy and his beard was sprouting again, but he looked ruddy and refreshed. Exchanging glances with his own reflection, he returned to his room and went to the window.

The sky was wrapped in a pale silvery haze. If he thought about it, this whole experience seemed completely unbelievable. Naked except for a pair of running shorts, he was standing in the middle of a room in the girls' dormitory. Like Apollo in Arcadia. Fantastic. Using reason to make sense of this situation seemed as impossible as photographing a dream. It was as if in falling into the river yesterday, he'd also fallen into a different world with completely different proportions and following a different logic.

Kamita returned. His suit looked brand new, his shirt was washed and ironed.

Five minutes later he said goodbye.

"So, at the bus stop at two o'clock."

"At two."

"I hope you won't forget."

She got up on the tips of her toes and put her hands on his shoulders. He kissed Kamita one more time, but less attentively somehow, already thinking about how there might be someone standing on the steps. As she walked out with him, Kamita looked like she might laugh.

He rushed downstairs and out of habit ran his fingers across his buttons and cuffs.

His handkerchief – also washed and ironed. His wallet. Knife. Ballpoint pen. Comb.

A piece of paper crunched in his outer side pocket.

Dear Sandris! Leave right away. I can't say any more right now, but it's very important. I'll write to you later and explain everything. Kamita, that nasty one, isn't who she claims to be. Don't believe a word she says. And, please, please, leave right away.

He read the sentences again, but couldn't bring himself to believe them. It was as though he was participating in a circus act in which he produced an aquarium filled with goldfish from his pocket.

Kamita, that nasty one, isn't … Don't believe a word she says.

It was written by the same hand as all the other letters, there was no doubt. If Marika were actually Kamita, then this handwriting had to be Kamita's. But it clearly wasn't, because only an idiot could think that Kamita would write something like this about herself.

When had the letter been slipped into his pocket? Yesterday? No, then the paper would have been soaked. So the letter had to have been put there recently. Right here in the dormitory. At Maṇa's – or whatever her name was.

Loosening his tie and unbuttoning his shirt collar he marched on, knowing only that the clarity that he thought was within his grasp had once again hopelessly evaporated.

13

"Young man, please come over here! Such a mess, such a mess…"

This plump guardian angel, a head in curlers shifting around in the window, was beckoning him to come over to her.

"You can't even imagine what I've had to go through because of you. A moment ago there was such a terrible commotion. That other person staying in your room showed up. Usually he disappears for several days in a row, who knows where he lives, who knows where he spends his time. But suddenly he was here and just started screaming, turning red."

A-ha! Probably about the cut-throat razor, he thought. That was to be expected…

"What was my neighbour unhappy about?"

"I've seen all kinds, but no one like him. You know I've been working here, thank God, for seventeen years, and there are a lot who like to scream or, let's say, write nasty comments in the book or threaten to complain. Usually, you can tell those sorts by their bitter and bloated faces. And, without fail, screaming right away. I deal with them easily: Don't scream, I say, remember where you are. This one, let me tell you, just a bum, buttons missing, collar warped. But his language, like he was an emperor. Looks in my eyes and flicks his finger against the windowpane: 'I'm giving you exactly five minutes to remove the person you put in my room. I booked a room, not a thoroughfare as a place to sleep in. Otherwise, I'll see to it myself, and throw his things out into the hallway.'"

"I don't have any things."

"Well, just a lunatic. Don't scream, I said, remember where you are, but he didn't listen. 'I've warned you, don't say later that you didn't know. If you like, you can complain to the *milicija*, to the public prosecutor's office, or to the Presidium of the Supreme Soviet itself.'"

So, it had nothing to do with the straight razor.

"Maybe that man is right? Maybe I really did sneak in illegally?"

"Good heavens, what are you saying? What do you mean, that man is right? I just don't know what to do now. Where should I put you?"

"Well, if he's wrong, then I'll stay right where I am."

The curlers bobbed as the woman nodded her head sceptically, the rosy skin of her scalp looked almost like that of a child as it shone through her thin, white hair.

"No, no, that won't work. I know people. He won't listen. Better to give him a wide berth. Who knows what else some-one like that might be capable of? Let the director herself get involved, but not me."

"Is he in the room?"

"Well, he took the key."

"I'll go up and take a look. Keeping in mind your keen advice..."

The guardian angel clapped together her fleshy palms.

"Please, just no trouble. We lose our bonuses if we have to call the *milicija*."

He went up the stairs, determined to feign ignorance. When he knocked there was only silence, though the door was unlocked. Maybe he didn't hear, he thought, so just to be sure he knocked again. Someone inside responded and he took that as a signal that he could enter.

There was no one in the first room.

In the second room, sitting at the table was – oh, to hell with it, what total nonsense – Gatiņš! Hunched over a chessboard, supporting his chin on both fists. There were chess pieces scattered around the room. He must have been playing against himself.

"Is that you, Gatiņš?"

"You could say that. Though there's good reason to question who any of us really is. At least until we show it through our works. In the worst case, through our words."

117

"Do you live here?"

"I try to live everywhere, wherever I am, according to the following formula: I feel, therefore I am. But in truth, one can question that too. To determine whether we are really living, we must first determine the meaning of life, but that has not yet been accomplished scientifically."

"And you wanted to throw my things out into the hall?"

Gatiņš blinked and studied him more carefully. "Why would you think that?"

"I didn't think it. The lady on duty just told me: I have to move out, free up the bed."

"Oh, that!" Gatiņš responded. "I apologise for my stupidity. This version of events never occurred to me."

"Me neither. I don't understand why you need a room at the hostel if you already have a house right here."

"Logical and clear. I don't need it at all."

"Of course, I'm neither a member of the *milicija* nor your wife. And the personal business of others doesn't interest me at all..." Then, trying to soften his sharp tone, he tried to chuckle. "You could've just told me. You didn't need to scare the old lady."

Gatiņš hunched his shoulders, listened calmly and, looking out from behind the thick lenses of his glasses, smiled like a figure from a Japanese painting.

"I'm very sorry," he added hesitantly after a long pause, "but you'll have to repeat this speech again, because, as far as I understand it, you're attributing actions to me which are in fact exclusively those of your old family friend, Professor Aparjods. A little patience, he'll return in a moment."

It seemed like a kind of icy delight, mixed with guarded reluctance, flashed across Gatiņš's half-closed eyes.

"I'll wager that he'll be as surprised as you."

"Aparjods?"

"Without a doubt."

"You mean, the professor doesn't know?"

"I'm sure of it. Otherwise I doubt he would've said, 'I'm

going to toss that joker right out the door.' I haven't yet determined why, but up until now he's displayed towards you an incomprehensible tenderness."

"In the end though what does it matter? The principle is important. Why does one person need two beds?"

"It's a matter of prestige. If a lion can't completely fill a cave himself, does that mean he'll let rabbits live there?"

"Aparjods is a lion in your understanding?"

"The professor has a very refined sense of prestige in any case. You don't have to ask him twice to tear a rabbit to shreds."

"There's no great art to tearing a rabbit to shreds."

"Believe me, he's an excellent representative of his genre, with amazing talent and a brilliant style."

"And if it turned out that there was a lion sleeping in the other bed too?"

"That would be especially interesting. Though this version is pure fantasy: in our era, lions are almost extinct. Take a seat, don't keep standing. The professor went to the telegraph office, he'll be right back."

Gatiņš, who was occupying himself with the chess pieces, lifted his eyes now and again. "Do you play chess?" he asked

"No. When I was a child, my father tried to teach me several times, but back then I was prejudiced against anything that required studying."

"But you play cards?"

"Also a no. A monotonous occupation."

"Do you know how to ride a motorcycle?"

"No..."

Gatiņš kept interrogating him.

"Then you don't like mathematics, chemistry or physics. You have no talent for learning foreign languages or grammar. You often lack initiative, endurance and organisation. You're rather indolent by nature and in some individual cases, frankly, even lazy. Isn't that right?"

"You apparently occupy your time with psychoanalysis?"

"I know this type well. To some extent, I could even say, from personal experience. For example, I learned to swim only in my twenty-second summer."

"That's not so late."

"Outwardly it's as if everything is fine and yet somewhere in the back of your mind, the thought – 'I don't know how' – begins, imperceptibly though systematically, to poison your heart as you begin to consider yourself to be bargain goods. Naturally, the 'knowers' move out in front, receive all the accolades, marry the prettiest girls, gain society's admiration, but you slink off to the side, slowly accepting your second-class position. It's as if you've imposed some kind of inferiority complex on yourself: Who am I to do that…"

"Interesting. How old were you when you learnt to play cards?"

"I haven't got round to cards yet. I became disgusted with myself too late. First I tackled learning English and the motorcycle. But to get a driver's licence with my eagle-eyed vision…"

He listened and focused his attention, unable to free himself from the suspicion that there was a trap hidden in Gatiņš's words. This turn in the conversation seemed dangerous. It was possible that Gatiņš was purposely exaggerating his own openness in order to provoke the same from him. It never did become clear from Gatiņš's words whether he was joking or speaking seriously.

"Well, that's the way things go," Gatiņš added.

"My watch has stopped, what time does yours say?"

"Do you have to hurry off somewhere again?"

"Not this time."

Gatiņš told him the time, looked at him, and then fell silent. Gatiņš must have been waiting for him to start speaking now.

A fly trapped in the curtain was buzzing mournfully at the window.

He sat down and straightened out the folds in the tablecloth.

"It's humid," Gatiņš said as he took his glasses off his pointed nose and used a handkerchief to wipe his forehead, which was fringed by his messy hair. "In the past they would've said, it's hay season."

"There's no hay season in the city. In Riga, at least, when the grassy patches are mowed along the canal, the clippings are left in small, fragrant stacks, but in Randava, I see, there's not even a proper square."

"But the hay machines from the collective farm do go along the street next to the jail wall. Though all they manage to do is clean the streets."

"But you don't clean them."

"I do. Everybody does."

"What does the groundsman do then?"

"You see, the groundsman doesn't clean them. After several different offices were combined, the groundsman also became the nightwatchman at the storehouse of the consumers' cooperative. He sleeps during the day. That's no surprise though, nobody can survive without sleep."

They both laughed.

"The groundsman cursed the administrator, I'd never seen anyone so angry before. And so he says, 'Please, fire me. Do you know of any other groundsman who's been fired for sleeping too much?' And he's right, of course. And anyway, who else would they hire? A state position can't remain vacant. And where's the guarantee that someone else would clean the streets…"

Gatiņš exhaled on to his glasses and began to polish them. Without glasses, his grimacing face looked unfamiliar, strangely empty and surprisingly weak.

Girls' voices fluttered in through the open window. The wind took the sound of the transistor radio and shredded it, scattering the pieces about like light and crinkly wood shavings.

Gatiņš was a blowhard and a blabbermouth, but it seemed like this time he was steering the conversation towards all kinds of trivialities. And he was hiding something. He clearly knew much more than he was letting on.

"So only young men are educated in your institute."

"Only young men."

"Are there any who, after getting out, decide to stay in Randava?"

"There are all sorts. Occasionally, a clever cuss might end up only looking back as he's led towards the gate. At that moment a person should be jumping for joy, and yet all this kid does is grumble like a Child of Israel in the desert: 'I'm not going to finish high school'…"

"Did you, by any chance, teach botany and zoology to someone named Žeņka?"

"To Žeņka?" Gatiņš, put on his glasses and ruffled his hair. "There are many Žeņkas. What would be his last name?"

"I don't know his last name. He works at the cemetery."

"Somehow I can't remember him."

"His girlfriend is Lība. Also a former criminal. Familiar to everybody around here."

"Žeņka?"

"I mean, Lība."

"I also know Lība. She even lived in our house for a while."

"After prison?"

"Your information isn't especially precise. Lība has never been in any prison. Definitely not. Of course, I haven't asked around, but I've got a little bit of experience in this area. A tailor knows his trade."

As he stood there, marking time, lost in his thoughts, Aparjods entered. He was in the same brightly coloured short-sleeved shirt that hung out over his pants. His oily brown face and massive, blunt neck were shiny. In one hand he was carrying a bottle of milk, in the other a loaf of sourdough rye.

"Well, here's the persona non grata," Gatiņš spoke first without any unnecessary introduction.

Aparjods, wheezing from his brisk walk, put the milk and

bread on the table. His face remained calm, with only a small hint of displeasure creeping on to his oval-shaped forehead.

"Occupant number two."

"Then I'm truly sorry," Aparjods's voice turned icy, then cutting. "I can't help you in any way. The administrator made a vulgar mistake and she must fix it."

"I've already been sleeping here for two nights." He tried to laugh. From the outside it probably sounded rather idiotic. Too often he laughed at the wrong times. This time, thank God, his laughter sounded more like he was showing off rather than attempting to convince Aparjods of anything or, even worse, pleading.

"That doesn't change anything. The room was taken. A deluxe suite can't be divided by beds, there is no such rule. If the state control showed up…"

"This hostel is overbooked."

"Not an excuse. If everyone doesn't get a pair of boots, that doesn't mean that you start selling boots individually."

"Surely … the administrator would have no objections to giving everyone their own deluxe suite."

"No way of knowing that. Sometimes difficulties are created on purpose." Aparjods made a chopping motion with his index finger as if it were a sword.

It's possible that pride was responsible for the feelings he subconsciously felt towards the metaphysical title of "professor", or perhaps it was the domineering and impatient way he was being spoken to, which excluded any possible arguments right from the start, nevertheless, as he stood in front of Aparjods, he felt himself shrinking. The criteria separating right and wrong for him, which only a moment ago had seemed so clear, no longer seemed stable or certain at all. And the idea of backing up his argument with such notions as right and wrong seemed completely absurd. Aparjods took what he needed, tore it apart, built it up again, and it all fitted perfectly. There could be no objection. Aparjods didn't argue, he put things in their rightful place, clarified misunderstandings and averted errors. Of course, his tone could offend sometimes and his sharp language provoke anger, but it was difficult to be angry with him, as his arguments were indisputable.

Aparjods, as always, was the master of the situation.

"Well, now you see," said Gatiņš, "the matter is resolved. Clear as can be."

"Bad behaviour comes as a result of lowered expectations. They convert the hostel into a factory dormitory and then are surprised that there aren't any rooms," the professor couldn't bring himself to stop yet, though he was now speaking much more calmly. "Go and tell them to give you a room of your own."

"If the worst comes to the worst," Gatiņš added, "my home is always at your disposal. There's a rollaway bed on the veranda and fresh hay in the stable loft."

"Thank you, I'm sure it will be fine."

"Well, what should we do," Gatiņš rubbed his hands together, "should we have a little party?"

"Not interested," Aparjods growled. "Playing chess and drinking liquor are two things that a respectable person does in the morning only on rare occasions."

"This morning could be such an occasion."

"The law must be respected."

"A wise man once said, 'The exception proves the rule.'"

"Oh, so for once you don't know the author of a quotation?"

"It's French proverb, it has no author."

"Nonsense, its author is Napoleon; a proverb gains an author when it's used by an authority."

"Then it would be better to say that it's by François-René de Chateaubriand. This phrase appears in his 1802 article on Christianity."

"Definitely not Chateaubriand. When it comes to laws, writers only blather on. Laws are given meaning by leaders."

"Fine," said Gatiņš, "let's assume you're right. Today, for a change, I don't feel like arguing. I have to go fishing tonight.

Why don't you come too? The heat is about to push my soul right out of my body."

"No."

"A law again?"

"No. My wife will be arriving on the midday train."

"And in the event of her not coming?"

Aparjods didn't answer.

He felt the professor's piercing stare and stirred suddenly. What was he waiting for? He was about to thrown out, and was standing there like a hypnotised rabbit, his mouth open, listening reverently to his every word. It would simply be rude to stay in that room any longer.

"Consider me to have moved out," he said.

"You're leaving already? But what about your things?"

"I don't have any things."

"Interesting, why did I think you had your things here?"

"No idea. Goodbye!"

14

Homeless again. But right now this concerned him very little. There's no sense troubling yourself with small things like that. As if he'd come here just to sleep on a coil mattress in a hostel. Naive little professor.

He was surprised that he actually felt fantastic – physically a bit tired, but in high spirits and with a remarkably rosy outlook on life.

His thoughts returned to Kamita and to last night. The magnifying glass of his recollection once again slid over this well-studied drawing, extracting various details from its shimmering interconnections, every streak and line uncovering new, surprising values.

It seemed like he could finally call himself a real man. Definitely. No two ways about it. With Vita it had just been fooling around. There was no comparison at all. And after that she'd disappeared, as if she'd fallen into a well. And sometimes it seemed like she'd never existed at all. Kamita is here and she'll be waiting for him again at two o'clock. At long last, he'd been enlightened by understanding what a woman really is. Until now it had just been a mythical concept which elicited in him confusion, low self-esteem and self-doubt. That had already begun when, as just a very small boy, he'd suddenly started to nurse some quite incomprehensible feelings towards Miss Zommere, the singing teacher. He began to have tempting dreams at night, but couldn't look her in the eye at school. He remembered how it had all begun: his class was on a field trip to the ethnographic museum, they were sitting on the grass eating sandwiches. Miss Zommere had taken off her shoes and stretched out her legs, which were hugged by translucent flesh-coloured stockings; when her dress inadvertently fell open just enough for him to see her suspender belt, he knew it was impolite to look, but continued to leer repugnantly all the while afraid that at any moment he'd be discovered and that this would be a terrible disgrace.

For years this incredible struggle continued within him – curiosity and shame, temptation and fear. He seemed to live in two worlds at once, shifting between torturous pain and thirst-driven hallucinations. In his imagination, he would usually have the role of some movie hero; he'd be self-assured, skilful, industrious and relentless, while in everyday life everything turned out differently. Where he needed to act, he'd doubt himself, and where he needed perseverance, he'd give up too easily. Courage was diluted by cowardice, quick-wittedness by confusion, nobleness by pettiness. His invariably beautiful plans would become depressing and humiliating over time, because he already knew beforehand how little they had to do with reality.

But now he had Kamita. This was complete reality. He had his own woman. Apparently he hadn't known himself very well and had judged himself too harshly. In any case, everything was in the best possible order, and he had no reason to complain about his own merits.

"And you really didn't know it was me?" Kamita had asked. The image that had grown out of the letter had become flesh and blood. That, of course, was a miracle that would take some getting used to. Ka-mi-ta. Kamita.

And right now some other words written down on paper wanted to mess this all up, to destroy it, undo it? What nonsense, it was ridiculous to even consider it.

But why were the letters written in handwriting that was clearly not Kamita's? Why had she signed them with Marika's name and sent Marika's photograph instead of her own? Terrific idiot. Worrying about a photograph when he actually had Kamita herself! That just didn't make sense. Just like it didn't make sense to turn everything into a game of handwriting analysis. What does it matter who wrote those letters?

The clock said twenty minutes to one.

At the post office a small elderly lady was selling dame's

violets. He bought the smallest bunch and pinned them to his shirt pocket.

It seemed pointless to wander around town for an hour and a half. He was stealing from himself. Another hour and a half, how awful!

But why couldn't he go over right now? Not to where they'd agreed to meet, of course, but to the dormitory; Kamita was surely counting down the minutes same as he was. Kamita wasn't afraid of bringing him inside at night. Awkward in front of the other girls? That's nothing. It definitely didn't seem like Kamita was trying to hide anything from her friends.

He continued to consider the situation and weigh up his options; meanwhile, his feet had already taken him all on their own to the dormitory. Struggling with himself for a moment, he chose to take a risk and follow his new-found sense of self-confidence right to where it had led him.

The stairwells were empty as always. For an instant he couldn't breathe, as if the air had been sucked out from between the walls. He bounded up the stairs, occasionally grabbing the banister with his right hand. The first turn, the second one, the third. Too many turns. The fourth. The fifth. The last one. The familiar door with the cracked door jamb.

He stopped, patted down his hair, and wet his lips. It was crazy, but he felt more nervous now than he did when he'd stood in front of this same door for the first time the morning before last. The light tap with his crooked finger against the door echoed in his chest as if it had been played over a loudspeaker.

She was already dressed up, but looked somehow different and unapproachable. He hadn't seen a hairstyle like that on her, so laboured over, so refined; her eyes coloured and staring at him with a proud brilliance. Her gaze, though, seemed totally impersonal, remembering nothing and understanding nothing. Was this even the same Kamita who had let him out this very door less than an hour ago? The magic of their proximity had been destroyed, everything had to begin anew. He froze as if he'd been driven into the ground, not knowing what to do.

"Oh, it's you. Did you forget something?"

Still, he couldn't hear any displeasure in her voice.

"Yes… a diamond ring. And some secret documents."

She laughed and took him by his lapels. He avoided looking into her eyes.

"At least not here in the hallway. Come inside."

"Maybe I'm disturbing you?"

"What shocking politeness…"

"I was thinking – the girls."

"None of them have shown up yet. You didn't see any of them downstairs?"

"Downstairs? Who, for example?"

"Biruta, for example. A moment ago when I was in the bathtub, I thought I heard knocking. The door wasn't locked, as Biruta is always forgetting her key."

Kamita let him into the front room, glanced out into the stairwell, and loudly slammed the door. The familiar smell of lilies of the valley wafted over him.

"I have an interesting piece of news to announce: I was thrown out of the hostel."

He couldn't come up with anything better in the spur of the moment; his completely unnecessary explanation ended up sounding like he was making excuses.

Kamita's eyes narrowed just barely.

"Does that mean that you're leaving?"

"I don't know… I'll have to think about it."

"Of course, it's not easy to find a room in Randava. But I have a few addresses. Still – *bon voyage*. Maybe it's better that way."

"You want me to leave?"

"No one can be kept by force."

"But if I stay…"

Kamita shot him a look laced with irony and laughed

129

quietly, "Then decide what you're going to do. And when you've decided – tell me."

"What would you like me to decide?"

"Whatever it is that you've already decided."

"It's not that simple."

"It's very simple. Everything should be done according to one's own free will. Did you ask for anyone's opinion when you came here?"

"I'm not asking for your opinion. I want to know."

"To know what?"

"Your thoughts."

"About what?"

She laughed again, this time more deeply, looking at him with slightly exaggerated confusion.

"About a lot of things."

He pulled out the letter guardedly.

"About this, for instance."

Kamita quickly read over its few lines and then stuffed the wrinkled paper back into his shirt pocket.

"What don't you understand? It's spelled out very clearly there: *Kamita is a villain, leave... Dear Sandris...*"

"Do you think so too?"

"My thoughts don't really matter right now."

"But what does matter then, really?"

"Whether you believe this letter or not. Anybody can write anything. Let's assume that it had been written differently: *Kamita is heavenly, stay.* Would that satisfy you?"

He felt better: she wanted him to stay, that was clear. The words she spoke had another meaning. Her words accumulated, piled on top of each other, and ground together like blocks of ice, but the direction of the current was clear.

"I'm interested in one thing: who wrote this letter?"

"Who?" Kamita looked intently into his eyes. "And what if it was me?"

"You?"

"Yes, so you'd have something to think about. But really, it was just an idiotic joke."

He didn't understand the meaning of the joke and Kamita also didn't explain it any more clearly. But he didn't want to go. He wanted to stay with Kamita. Why did they talk so much about leaving? It seemed like in that they'd found a real point of contention.

He should just say that he's going to stay and that's that. An hour ago it would've been simple to do that, but now something held him back. And this was a different Kamita. Shame, shyness, fear, doubt. Really they didn't know each other at all. Barely at all.

"Fine, let's not get petty. After all, the evening is still far off."

"Have you had anything to eat? I can heat up some soup in the kitchen."

"Thanks, I've already eaten, but maybe you have a razor I could shave with."

"I only have manicure scissors."

"Did Marika know you were writing to me?"

"Marika? I'm sure she did. Why wouldn't she know? We all live so close to each other..."

Kamita appeared to pick a small piece of fluff off of his lapel.

"And Biruta also knew?"

"I think so."

"Why did you send Marika's photograph?"

Kamita continued working calmly on his clothing, patting down his shoulders, tightening is necktie.

"If you want to know, if it's so important to you – we all wrote the first letter together. Just for the fun of it."

"I see."

"Are you satisfied now? The last train to Riga leaves a few minutes after 10 tonight."

"Are you hurrying off somewhere?"

"No, I meant – you."

131

"Yes, you."

"No – you."

He raised his hands and Kamita slapped his palms, he caught her fingers, she pulled away and hit him again.

"You."

"No – you."

The words had no meaning. But the transparent wall of unfamiliarity, which had risen up between them and warped their images, scattered suddenly like fog in the wind. They were together again, nothing separated them. They held each other's hands tighter, they sought and found the missing paths to each other. You could see it in their eyes: the recaptured courage, they were no longer afraid, but welcoming. They stood closely pressing against each other, their breath joining them, entwining them.

"Sandris, listen, we don't have time."

"Yes, we do."

"We don't. We have to meet at two…"

"What does your watch say?"

"I don't know, it stopped."

Someone knocked on the door.

"Biruta is here, right on the dot."

"Let her keep knocking, she'll get bored and leave."

"That would be rude of us. To make her stand by the door all day and night."

"Wait here, I'll go and look."

The knocking continued without stopping, piercing, relentless.

"Kamita, this time you'll let me in, don't pretend, I know you're there. You're just afraid of showing yourself to me, that's why you've crawled off trembling into a corner. Let me in!"

It was hard to mistake that sharp, somewhat hoarse voice for anyone else's. It belonged to Lība.

Kamita stopped and froze mid-step, but Lība kept rattling the door handle.

"You're wicked, you're a coward, do you hear! Let me in! I brought the letters, I'll show you what he wrote to me. You won't get away with it this time!"

He also walked towards the front room. Kamita shot him an icy stare and gestured for him to go back. He didn't move. A loose board creaked under his feet. Although standing outside, Lība must have heard it, as she began rattling the handle even more angrily.

"Kamita, don't pretend. I can see you. You're standing right there. Are you really too much of a coward to open the door? You knew he didn't come here to see you…"

Kamita shot him another piercing look as if she were making sure that he'd heard everything; her eyes were wide-open and questioning, but also angry, confused, and spiteful. The door shook lightly like the top of a sprung trap, there was no sense in staying quiet any longer. Kamita finally made up her mind and laughed with contempt. Her white teeth flashed in the half-light. He looked in the mirror on the wall and calmly, too calmly, fixed his hair.

"Go away, don't clown around. I'd love to let you in, but Sandris hasn't gotten dressed yet."

"You're lying! I saw, he left. Never, do you hear me? He's never coming back to you!"

The door handle was still moving. But slower now. Lība spoke in whispers, quickly and through tears.

"Well, well. That's interesting, why?" asked Kamita.

"Because you're a cheat. That's why I'll never let you have him. You didn't even know that there was a Sandris in this world. You spent a night together, that doesn't mean a thing. When Egils left for the army, you only needed a week to trade him for Žeņka. And after that, Žeņka for Viktors.

"This is starting to get boring. Can't you give your performance a rest? You'll feel better too. Or I'll tell Sandris right away…"

"What? What are you going to tell him? He knows me better than you. Look at all of his letters. He came here to see me."

"Maybe he came here to see you, but he ended up with me."

"He never would've done that if he'd known the truth."

"What truth? That you've been in jail? Or that you have a child?"

He didn't wait any longer, it was horrible to stand there in silence; he went up to the door and pressed the lock button. Kamita tried to get in his way and stop him, but her resistance only increased his determination.

The door burst all the way open.

Lība moved as if she'd been brutally shoved, turned deathly white, and stepped back confused. She had a large packet of letters in her left hand, in their familiar yellow envelopes. Bending her elbow, she lifted her right hand in front of her face, as if she were protecting herself, and moved her body in a strange way as if she were dodging something.

"No, no. Go to Kamita, go, go. You heard what she said."

"Yes, I heard…"

"Well, good. Then everything's clear."

"I think it is." Kamita's beautiful face twisted with contempt. Something flashed across it that he'd never noticed before, and to see it was unpleasant, even horrible. It was as if her face had flaked off, revealing a void with a beautiful set of white teeth glimmering at him from within it. "Is there anybody here who doesn't already know it? Maybe we should call some witnesses? Good, let's do it!"

Lība's gaze became intense and piercing It shot right through him and it was impossible to bear. She shifted towards him with an almost imperceptible motion.

"Of course, of course. Don't believe her, Sandris, don't believe her," Kamita laughed.

Lība's hands dropped and the yellow envelopes scattered across the steps.

"Alright then… Everything's clear…"

The scattered letters looked like autumn leaves when she ran through them and down the stairs. She didn't look back.

He was so shocked that he didn't even understand what was happening: why was Lība running, why was he running after her?

She stumbled up to the door, but it was locked. She pulled open a window and wrenched herself up on to the windowsill. She'd climbed up like that once before, it seemed like he'd seen all this already. He just didn't understand why. Why?

And then Lība was gone, no longer on the sill. Kamita screamed and ran up to the window. He looked out too. A white shirt was swaying softly as it dried on Lība's balcony. But Lība herself was lying on her back in the flower bed, surrounded by the whitewashed bricks placed around its edges.

15

He didn't really understand his place in everything that had just happened or what it all meant. That he and Liba could have had anything in common seemed surreal. Liba was behind ten parentheses, somewhere very far away, separate and alone. Liba? Why Liba? How could it be Liba? He was immediately overcome by a piercing awareness of his responsibility – *But what if it's your fault?*

He knew as much as any of the others, but they, for some reason, were looking at him.

She fell.

Why did she climb up on to the windowsill this time?

She wanted to get to the balcony. She had that habit.

That seemed so dumb, so misguided, that he couldn't even take it seriously. His feelings of awkwardness confirmed his guilt even more clearly. Why was it that he preferred an easy lie to admitting the truth? Who was he thinking about more – Liba or himself? Maybe he was inadvertently trying to cover his trail in order to appear cleaner and more innocent than he really was? Really, why? And yet, no ... he had nothing to do with what happened. If only he'd had even the slightest sense...

She was lying there with her eyes open, still, quiet. Her mouth looked unnaturally large and red. Later he noticed that there was a small trickle of blood connecting one nostril to her lips. Her palm felt warm just as if she were still alive, but she had no pulse. He tried to lift her arm; it seemed unnaturally heavy and began to bend in a place it shouldn't have.

Fortunately an ambulance soon arrived. People were crowding around, trampling the scrawny pansies, they shoved past him and out in front. He was gradually pushed further back. That was a relief of a sort. He wasn't forced to keep looking at Liba's face. No one noticed him any more, the gazes of the curious onlookers were fixed on the doctor and the orderly. He was just part of the crowd, just a passer-by who'd been drawn into this crush of people by chance. No, he didn't run away and abandon Lība, he had simply been pushed to the side.

After Lība had been lifted into the ambulance, he summoned up his courage and fought his way to its half-closed doors.

"I could ride along… If necessary…"

The doctor was young, with a carefully separated parting in his butter-yellow hair.

"Are you a relative?"

The drifting stares of the crowd latched on to him again and began to drain him.

"No, just concerned."

"There's no need. Come to the hospital later."

"In how long?"

The doctor shrugged his shoulders.

The ambulance drove off. The crowd gradually began to scatter. A *milicija* officer walked up, wiping the sweat from his brow. He held a leather-covered board, its long cord tightly wrapped around his left hand.

"They say you saw it happen."

"Yes."

"Just in case, I'll write down your address. First name, last name, where do you live?"

He responded automatically, without even thinking about it.

"What are you doing in Randava?"

"Nothing. I just came to see it."

The *milicija* officer stopped writing and muttered something.

"Where do you work?"

"Currently, nowhere."

"You were visiting the dormitory?"

"Yes, visiting."

"Did you spend the night?"

"I came half an hour ago."

"To see whom?"

"An acquaintance."

"Documents?"

"I don't have a passport."

"No matter, show me what you have."

The *milicija* officer gave him back his documents and tapped his fingers against the bill of his cap in a perfunctory manner.

"Is that all?"

"Yes, well, you know, I'm just crossing my t's and dotting my i's. During a cold snap this spring, some lads at a party put a girl in the attic to, let's say, help her sober up a bit, and then forgot about her. But, well, she didn't wake up, she froze to death. It's a good thing I'd written down their addresses: one young guy from Riga, another from Liepāja, supposedly guests, supposedly friends. Try finding them later on."

"Thank you."

"Yes, well, just in case, you can never know how things turn out. Some things start out as a big joke, but end up being quite serious."

He noticed Kamita further off, she was standing by the corner of the building and was possibly waiting for him, but he pretended not to see her and went off in the other direction.

He couldn't clear his mind: jumbled thoughts kept churning away, turning round and round in his head. They weren't even whole thoughts, just individual confused phrases.

The torn remains of old advertisements flapped against the noticeboard, one behind the other in many layers, blue, green, white – the words mixed together, creating nonsensical rebuses. Everything was twisted, broken and disgustingly grey: the concrete pavement slabs, the paint-flecked fences, the old building's walls. Cigarette butts littered the dusty gutters, together with crumpled bus tickets and all kinds of trash. The street was empty and pointlessly long.

He had walked here once before – back then he'd wanted to leave. What kept him here?

Sometimes they think – a joke, but then...

No, he wasn't careless. It was more that he was credulous. From separate details he'd managed to patch together, he'd created a kind of ideal image, a fantasy, and had come to believe it. Pygmalion the Second. It all fitted so nicely and connected so beautifully. Like in an operetta.

When those damned letters first began arriving, he'd undergone a transformation that was literally visible to the eye, he'd become a completely different person. Even the master sergeant of his company had noticed it and begun to sniff the air suspiciously, thinking that he might have started drinking.

The photograph had become worn from frequent handling; later he didn't even need to take it out of his pocket, at night, standing guard, or during breaks, while lying down in the lawn by the firing range, he would still see her face anyway. And he could hear what she was telling him: sometimes whispering bashfully, other times happily and with excitement or also dejectedly with pained sighs.

And then finally the truth – what he'd accepted as reality turned out to be an illusion. Everything came tumbling down, there was no sense in trying to comfort himself. The layers upon layers of illusions were joined by nothing, each one flapped separately like the colourful shreds pinned to the noticeboard. The face he saw in his dreams had no connection with the body he'd touched. That body lived on a completely different plane and knew nothing about the words that echoed in his ears. But those words had been written by Lība...

Old Mārtiņš, by the kvass barrel in the station square, recognised him right away.

"Well hello, so, you're still in Randava. Though I see yesterday didn't do you any good."

"No good at all."

"You look a bit more drawn in the face. Well, that's understandable, Saturdays and Sundays are the hardest days for
young people. But after that there's a whole week for rest.
Another small one?"

"Please."

"Yes, yes, after a dance, kvass tastes pretty good. First of
all, because sprats want to swim; second, the body has lost
all its fluids – just like it had been in a sauna."

"Let's not talk about any dances."

"Bad moods can occur. Best not to take everything so
seriously. But matters of love are important, especially when
you're young. If things go wrong for an old buck like me, I
think of it like this: it's easy to blame others, but it's not like
you're some kind of a saint. Isn't that right?"

"Keep pouring, you old saint, and don't talk so much." A
sullen old woman stuck out her cup. "Don't mix up young
people's heads."

"It's not so easy to do that. They might believe there was
kvass around when we were young, but imagining that we
went to dances in our day, that's too much for them."

There was a contingent of funeral guests at the bus stop.
Black dresses, black socks, black scarves, thick, dark suits. A
large man was standing and bending forwards while holding a
wreath in one hand and a cake wrapped in a cloth in the other.

Why did she jump? Crazy Lība. She knew what she was
doing. It was on purpose, clear as day. And what would've
changed if he'd listened and left earlier? What had she
wanted? That they'd never met? Or – mostly – that he
wouldn't have stayed with Kamita? One way or another,
it was absurd. Too many lies. Everything would come out
anyway.

Somehow they were alike after all. Like Old Mārtiņš said,
it's easy to blame others, but you're not any kind of a saint
either.

He went into the station and looked at his watch, time
was dragging on at a fiendishly slow pace. In the corner of

the station hall a Turkmen dressed in a long cotton robe was sleeping stretched out on a wooden bench with a rolled up carpet under his head. An infant was crying monotonously next to his mother's breast. A boy and girl were laughing rapturously about something, not loudly but it had brought them to tears, shaking and wheezing; gradually stopping, calming down, but as soon as their gazes met, starting all over again.

The door was heavy and continued swinging for a long time after being let go.

A taxi drove up, a bearded sailor from the fishing fleet got out. The driver started to eat a sandwich.

"Are you available?"

"Where to?"

He sat down next to the driver.

"To the mortuary."

The driver shot him an inquisitive look and switched off the mumbling on the radio.

The mortuary was located on the far side of town, right by the cemetery. The small one-storey construction looked quiet and empty, and there was a sign in the window that said "Closed on Sundays". In the yard there was a shack and a large pile of boards, and right next to these there was a stack of several concrete borders for graves. At the other end of the building there was a flower bed. He went in through the small gate and rapped on the nearest window. A dog appeared from the shack and started to bark lazily. A moment later a sleepy old man appeared, covered head to toe in wood shavings.

"What do you want? There's nobody here today."

"There's a Žeņka working here, would you know by chance where he lives?"

The old man thought about it for a while, sighed heavily and shook his head.

"First I've heard of it. I've got no idea. Cigūzis, Boķis, and Zilpaušs work in digging, Urbaste and Limping Viļumsons in carpentry."

"He's the cashier."

"Emma works at our cash register."

"Well, it's possible then that it's someplace else. A young person, twenty, twenty-five years old."

"Oh my, then it won't be here. We're all old, all old. I'm practically the youngest."

"Might there be another mortuary in Randava?"

"Haven't heard of one."

He went back out on to the street. The taxi hadn't left yet.

"Where to now?" asked the driver.

"Doesn't matter. To the centre... No, to the hospital."

The driver wrapped his sandwich in paper and started the car.

As they drove the sun was shining right into their faces; he grimaced and closed his eyes. Violet streaks and black dots danced across his vision. The car's tyres thumped monotonously across the round cobblestones.

Patients in pajamas and flannel robes were sitting on benches by the greenery out in front of the hospital, chatting with visitors. Open windows. Pale faces eagerly waiting. Crutches. Limbs in casts. White gauze bandages.

A terrible place. One had only to step into its medicated halls for the world to turn into Dante's *Inferno*. Everyone had something wrong with them, everyone was sick, decaying, wasting away, moving back and forth like on a precarious pendulum between life and death. It seemed like there wasn't a single healthy person left on the face of the earth. He, fortunately, had never had to spend time in the hospital. Would his living flesh also be sliced open someday, flayed apart, and sewn back up again; a doctor with rubber-gloved hands rummaging around his insides, sawing his bones, and pulling at his veins? Huh. Usually, it was all somewhere far away, outside of his awareness.

The nurse on duty studied the papers in front of her at length whilst making phone calls.

"You'll have to wait."

"Here?"

"No, go to the operation room."

The words "No Unauthorised Entry" were lit up above the opaque glass doors. At the end of the hallway, next to a sickly rubber tree, there were several completely innocent-looking chairs. Like those in Kamita's room at the dormitory.

A half hour later, the doctor came out through the white doors. Young, clumsy and on the heavy side, with a thick moustache over his soft, pink upper lip. The doctor, turning one of the chairs round and sitting with his arms resting on the chair's back, lit a cigarette.

"I don't have any news for you, we don't know anything yet."

"Is she alive?"

"We don't operate on the dead, we perform autopsies on them."

"I mean... is there hope?"

The doctor blew a smoke ring and turned towards him, giving him a sombre, tired look.

"She hasn't regained consciousness."

"But just in general..."

"There are no 'general' cases in medicine, only specific ones."

A woman entered the hallway carrying a towering stack of packages and hesitated for a moment in the doorway before moving a few steps closer to the doctor. She studied him inquisitively and, meeting his gaze, suddenly dropped all the bundles on to the floor. She covered her face with both hands and began to weep quietly.

"What's wrong?" The doctor jumped up. "Are you looking for someone?"

"I came for a visit... I thought she'd be home... but they told me she'd been brought here..."

"Are you Marcinkēviča's mother?"

"Isn't she here?"

The woman wiped the tears from her nose with her rough fingertips.

Her mother… That was immediately clear. Except Lība looked round, and her mother had a more heavy-set squarishness to her, perhaps because she was taller.

"Please sit down, your daughter is here. But we don't know anything yet. We just have to wait."

"Fine, I'll wait," the woman nodded in agreement as she shuddered into a new round of tears. "I'll wait."

He got up; he felt like someone was gripping him by the throat.

"I'll come back later," he said.

Meeting Lība's mother, that's all he needed. He just wasn't up to it. No one could ask that of him. He hated tears. Tears sapped his strength, made him soft and weak. In the past, if anyone started crying, he'd immediately start up too. He had no idea how to comfort her. And what could he possibly say to her?

You see, I'm also here because of your daughter.

And who are you?

Nobody, a stranger, but I was there when it happened.

You don't know each other?

No, we wrote letters to each other. That is – just please understand me right – this happened because of me…

She's no fool after all. No, no, he couldn't talk to her.

It was good to be on the street. Everything feels like it's behind you. Or maybe in front. At least, further away.

Lība wasn't normal… And doing this to herself, on purpose… But what if it wasn't on purpose? What if in all the excitement her foot slipped?

Now there couldn't be any thought of leaving. And where would he go? Maybe he should go and sit in the garden out front? He remembered the riverside with its delights and desire. There are enviable people, after all, who don't have to solve riddles, who, with a calm mind and without the least bit of mental anguish, are spending time on the riverbank right now, swimming without a care in the world, cheerfully throwing around beach balls. A beautiful, tempting dream.

Biruta and Caune, Marika and Tenisons are probably on the riverbank. And then the rest of the girls too. The curious looks, the facetious remarks all flashed before his eyes. No, thank you.

Staying there remained agonisingly difficult, he had to move, to do something; he walked off without any destination, straight up the first street he passed. The town continued to thin out, cows mooed, chickens clucked, the sun flashed its shimmering rays through the canopy, crickets chirped and birds sang. The grain fields were undulating on the other side of the overgrown roadside ditch.

A locomotive manoeuvred along the railroad tracks, puffing rhythmically, the piles of railway sleepers smelt of pitch.

And then he was back into town. Evening approached, the sun burned red over the roofs of buildings. He was standing in the square by the bus station. A crackling voice announced the bus from Randava to Mazsalaca. Drowsy students on a school trip sat with their heads hanging down, yawning, and looking around indifferently. A long-haired youth said goodbye to a girl smiling bashfully. Old women were sitting on the bench with empty baskets.

Suddenly he saw Lība's mother. Practically next to him. It seemed as though her eyes saw nothing. But what if she recognised him after all? Her gaze was directed right at him. He instinctively nodded his head.

No answer. But now that he'd acknowledged her, he couldn't just walk away, he had to say something. They were standing too close to each other. She definitely saw. There's no way she couldn't have seen.

He wanted to run away again. As always.

"Excuse me… I'm sorry… Did they let you in to see Lība?"

She winced and then looked around for some reason.

"Yes."

"Did she say anything?"

Lība's mother shook her head, brushing her lips with her fingers.

"The doctor didn't let her."

"Are you leaving?"

She nodded, gnawing at the tips of her fingers.

"I have to go. How could I have known... how could it even occur to me? The cow's by itself. The house is empty. I have to arrange for someone to help."

He was hoping the conversation would end then, what else could there be for them to say to each other, but Liba's mother took out her handkerchief, blew her nose, and started to talk about her troubles.

"The traffic is good right now, but it's still pretty far away. And I'm always up to my neck in work. I hardly get a chance to visit her. Last time was around New Year. But last night, it felt like someone said to me, 'You have to go today.' Just that kind of feeling. I thought, I have the day off, I'll come and see how she's doing. I'll bring something to eat, the other week I slaughtered a calf. I got on the bus, but the whole time my heart felt like something was not right, not right."

She had the same kind of short, blunt nose that Liba did and when they spoke they both moved their lips in exactly the same way, pushing them out just a little bit. Not a hint of gypsy roots. It would be hard to imagine a more Latvian face.

"But who's staying with the child?"

"With what child?"

"I mean, Liba's child."

Hints of definition appeared across her slack, indistinct face, surprise flared up in her eyes, and her forehead arched in confusion.

"What... Why would Liba have a child? From when? Heaven forbid."

"Doesn't Liba have a child?"

"Can you imagine? Where would she have got a child? She's practically a child herself. Still going to school not long ago."

Her eyes studied him with growing disquiet, but her voice was tired.

146

"Bad luck, bad luck... I'll try to come back tomorrow, but only if I can arrange for someone to fill in for me."

"I'm sure your neighbours can look after the house."

"The house, sure, but who'll do the work?"

"I'm sure they'll find someone at the collective farm."

She sighed and shook her head.

"But I don't work at the collective farm. I work at the cemetery."

"At the cemetery?"

He must have shown his surprise for too long. But really what was he, this silly man, so amazed about?

"It's not as strange as it sounds. Work is work: hiring diggers, documents, tending and watering the plots."

"Do you live at the cemetery?"

"Yes. We've been undertakers for three generations now. I didn't want to do it back in my day, but that's how it turned out: the Germans shot my father, later on Lība and I ended up alone. I thought – where will we go, how will we live? At least we have a roof over our heads and work as well. And how could we leave Granny... It was probably the wrong choice. I should've left, at least for Lība's sake. She ended up having to suffer a great deal. I knew it from my own childhood. In school, you're called to the front of the class and they ask, 'Where do your parents work?' 'At the graveyard.' Everybody laughs, makes fun. Nobody wants to be your friend, to come over. Once I woke up at night and heard Lība crying in bed. I asked her what was wrong. She said, 'The boys call me the Corpse Queen.' Later, of course, she became wiser, but still, you know, those kinds of things leave a mark on your heart; Lība was very sensitive. She never really had any friends..."

"Was Lība's father German?"

"Heaven forbid, why would he be German?"

Oh Lord, why was he pestering this unfortunate woman so much? But it seemed like Lība's mother wasn't angry with him – quite the opposite, she even seemed happy that she could open her heart to him.

"It'll be two years this autumn since Liba left us, after finishing high school. But we've barely seen each other lately! After ninth year she went to live at the boarding school. I waited for her to come on Saturdays. Nothing. She calls: 'Mum, I've got no time.' The autumn and winter nights are unpleasant here, dark and empty all around, the trees swaying, the wind howling. In the spring and summer it's a completely different picture, then it's nice at the cemetery, just like a park. But after secondary school it seemed like it had to happen that way regardless – even without that bad turn."

"What bad turn?"

"Didn't you know? She'd gotten it into her head to become a doctor. Was studying like crazy. It was a huge blow for her."

"Oh, I see…"

"Well, yeah. A girl. A boy with the same marks was taken instead. She never even came home when she returned from Riga. She stayed in Randava and, hot on the heels of all that, started working at the factory. Didn't you know?"

"No."

"She took it very badly. She didn't say much even to me, but I know her. And now this…"

She opened her purse and began digging around inside of it. He thought she might be looking for a handkerchief to wipe the tears from her cheeks, but instead she pulled out a mashed-up packet of cigarettes.

"Do you smoke?"

"No, thank you."

"Liba doesn't want me to smoke," she said gesturing dismissively.

The cigarette didn't want to burn in her wet fingers. She eagerly took a drag, but tears kept streaming down her cheeks.

"You're probably from the factory too?"

"Yeah… In a sense…"

"How did it happen?"

"If only someone could say… She was standing on the

windowsill. It was so sudden… It looked like she wanted to climb up on to the balcony."

"Terrible… terrible…"

She crumpled up the cigarette and cried softly as she turned to her side.

Passengers started to be let on to the bus.

"Well, I have to go," she said.

"Good night then. I'll be waiting for you. You told me so much…" he wanted to add "interesting information", but stopped himself just in time. Idiot, really an idiot.

"If only she could pull through."

"Why can't she…"

She looked down, sighed, and walked away.

Standing as if frozen, he watched her leave, feeling his long-forgotten childhood fear of blinking his eyes. At the same time, though still anxious, he felt overwhelming peace in understanding more than he had before. And all of a sudden he wanted to cry too.

16

The bus had left, but he was still sitting on the bench, with a hazy sense that as soon as he got up, he'd need to go somewhere and do something. As to where he should go and what he should do – he had no idea. He had to think a little more, get himself together, consider what he'd heard, and then he'd finally understand it all and would be able to make a decision. But he wasn't really even thinking, just killing time. He'd delayed his walk to the hospital, and his plans and decisions from earlier still lay ahead of him. But honestly he just couldn't do any of it yet. It was more than he could take right now. At least right then when the inside of his head felt like a hazy void.

What would he even say to Lība? *I'm sorry that it turned out this way, a silly misunderstanding, now I know the truth.* Ridiculous. The truth was that he always thought about himself, with absolutely no consideration for anyone else. Me. Mine. When he'd received Lība's letters, he'd only thought about himself. And coming here, he'd also only thought about himself, his pride and appearance. And he interpreted everything with ghastly simplicity: in his egotistical blindness he reduced serious human relationships to naked schemes, dry mathematical formulas, in which even the love games with Kamita fitted perfectly after an equals sign.

Of course, he wasn't psychic and couldn't have immediately guessed the identity of the actual letter writer. But to at least consider what was written in them… He'd been in such a rush, so terribly afraid that his trip would be in vain.

Pitiful and sad. A repulsive betrayal on his part. Regardless of whether it was Lība or someone else.

And how easily he'd believed the legend of Lība's ruined past. While letting Gatiņš's words go over his head. He now knew that people believe what they want to believe, and he'd been no different. But Lība advertised her own vices far too much and carried them around like flags flapping on a parade. She was still crazy. Why did she need to lie like that?

The taxi turned off the main road and stopped in front of the bus station. The new arrival's stooped and wobbly gait was very familiar. Only the white shirt and bright necktie seemed unusual.

Aparjods took a few steps and stopped as if he couldn't decide in which direction he was heading. Then, tugging at his trousers and buttoning his coat, the professor came towards him. Noticing him, he stopped again and furrowed his brow with dissatisfaction.

"Ah. You're here? When does the bus arrive?"

"What bus do you mean?"

"From Riga."

"From Riga? I really don't know."

"I thought – you also…"

"No, for no reason. Does it arrive soon then?"

"I think so: at twenty-five past."

Aparjods walked up to the schedule and, after studying it for a long time, glanced at his watch.

"In ten minutes," he said, sitting down next to him on the bench. "This is a very comfortable bus, it leaves Riga a half hour after the train. If you're late for the train sometimes…"

"Yes, it's very comfortable."

She'd written that spring that she was working, that her shadow was shrinking, and that it seemed to her that the time left until summer was also shrinking. After that he'd also noted the length of his shadow every day as he walked around the asphalt courtyard by the barracks. It was wearing down incredibly slowly. Sometimes he tried to imagine her shadow next to his, but that image was indistinct and different every time. Now he saw that shadow very clearly.

"Did they give you a room?"

"A room?"

"At the hostel earlier?"

"Ah. No. I didn't even ask."

"Are you going to leave?"

"No. I don't know. Maybe."

Since she was unconscious, at least she didn't feel pain. The doctor said it was too early to know anything. His evasive response probably meant that the worst could still happen. But what did "the worst" mean? Could there be anything worse than what had already happened?

The professor was sitting spread out, looking extremely sure of himself and his position, his knees pointing to each side, his stomach thrust out, both arms thrown back and supported by the back of the seat. But his gaze was timid and evasive.

"...But it wouldn't be any surprise if the bus were late today. Sunday night. A crush of people at every stop, the time it takes for one group to get off and the other on..."

To talk about the bus schedule right now seemed unnatural and strange; he felt a barely constrained feeling of resentment towards the professor. But looking over he saw that Aparjods wasn't even waiting for an answer. The professor wasn't speaking so much to him as to himself. And he looked tired: heavy bags hung from beneath his eyes, his face was oily and shiny, he was wheezing, his chest heaved sharply with the rest of his body after each exhalation.

"Or it might not be late at all, the road is good."

"There's a speed limit, so what does it matter?"

Right at that moment Marika and Tenisons appeared by the bus station building.

"Marika, look! What an extremely pleasant surprise! The poet, in the flesh. I thought so. Randava is a small town after all."

Marika showed no hint of happiness.

"Good evening, we were already looking for you at the hostel," he said, shooting a quick glance which seemed to say nothing.

"Is there any news on Lība?"

"You were there yourself."

"But how is she now?"

Marika shook her shoulders. "No news. Biruta went over there a short while ago."

"There's no sense talking about Liba," Tenisons's eyes shot back and forth observantly and returned again and again to Marika. "A crazy person can't help but behave in a crazy way. Nothing good was going to come of any of it anyway."

Tenisons was behaving very strangely. Or, to be more precise, very mysteriously. He had a smile on his face, but didn't shake hands.

"Well, it's nice that we ran into each other here. Really wonderful…"

Marika turned away with a grimace.

"I'm so sorry, but I have to go now," she said.

"Go?" Tenisons's head snapped towards her. "Nonsense. The bus will be here soon."

"Let it come."

"Five minutes and the bus will be here."

"Are you waiting for somebody?"

"Not really. But there's always a chance someone might come."

Tenisons rubbed his hands together and studied Aparjods. The professor seemed not to hear Tenisons's words and was looking in the direction of the gas station, showing no desire to participate in the conversation.

There was a threat of some kind hiding in Tenisons's voice. What did "there's always a chance someone might come" mean? Tenisons was definitely waiting for somebody and wanted him to be there when they met.

"What did you do today?" asked Marika. "Did you finally solve your crossword puzzle? You were probably very surprised?"

He couldn't imagine Liba writing the letters. He couldn't imagine Liba in the hospital.

The large clock on the wall wasn't giving the correct time. His watch said two minutes after.

"It's really good that we ran into each other. A little while ago I started wondering if you'd already left."

"We were playing ball on the riverside and suddenly Valda ran up screaming: 'Friends, Lība's dead. She jumped out the window. Out of jealousy.'"

"The big clock is wrong."

"A minute either way, maybe a good friend will arrive. Let's say, a miracle happens. Maybe a mutual acquaintance or…"

"Varis, stop it! No offence, but you're really one to talk. I wouldn't be surprised if you jumped out of a window yourself."

The smile on Tenisons's lips twisted a little bit.

"Thanks, sweetheart. I'm sure I won't be doing that. During my military service one of our guys fell from the tower, overall he was pretty lucky, there were some young spruces growing below, not a scratch on him, he just started to stutter a bit."

"Don't trouble yourself, if you're in a hurry…"

"Calm down. He's staying."

Suddenly he was overcome by a terrible suspicion. He sensed something now. Tenisons also became serious; his mask changed from one of saccharine friendliness to the way a boxer stares over his raised fists – sharp, tensed, and coldly calculating.

His heart shuddered, his vision became hazy, his neck began to pulse, still he forced himself to hold Tenisons's gaze and not look away. Tenisons couldn't be allowed to read anything into his face. At least nothing that he was waiting for or hoping to see.

"Let's just say that we're organising a meeting with the poet Sandris Draiska. OK?"

"Varis, stop! Lība wrote those letters. Isn't that enough for you?"

"After everything that's happened, it's more important than ever… Look, the bus is coming!"

"Fool…"

"It'll be alright, little mouse. Don't worry."

He hadn't been expecting this kind of a twist. Tenisons was clearly taunting him, but he didn't know how to respond. He was standing silent as a post. But it could be that it was better this way. In a moment it will all be clear. In a moment we'll see…

The bus stopped and in an instant was enveloped by a crowd. Those who'd been waiting impatiently clustered round it. Crumpled, tormented, overheated passengers flowed out of the bus in waves with bags, suitcases, and packages. Baby carriages shot out like shells from the end of a cannon. Guitars, wilted flowers, tree branches flowed along on this stream of people.

"Let's get closer," said Tenisons, "I can't see anything from here."

The crowd gradually thinned out. The last one to get out was an old grandmother with a hen tied into a basket, clucking and moving its head around. The driver walked around the bus and checked the tyres. The cashier closed her window.

"You know, I don't see him," Tenisons's shoulders sagged.

Marika turned her back demonstratively to the bus. Tenisons continued to look around.

"Nothing… Well, isn't that a joke."

Their gazes collided again.

"You seem to have been wrong."

"No way of knowing that yet."

"Let's go," said Marika, "no sense standing here. You tried showing off and you failed, that's enough. Are you also going to the centre?"

"No" he said, "I'm going to the station."

"You're leaving?"

He didn't answer.

"Let's go." Marika started tugging Tenisons by the arm.

"One second…"

Tenisons lit a cigarette, took a puff, and then smirked contemptuously. "Just a few more words, my dear poet. You see, I was looking for you at the hostel…"

"Yes, so you said."

"I asked if, by chance, a certain Aleksandrs Draiska wasn't staying with them. They said that there wasn't…"

"That's right. I checked out at noon."

"That wasn't today, but yesterday morning."

"Very interesting."

"My thoughts exactly," Tenisons said, lingering on each syllable. "But I, if you remember, found you. I guess I've got a pretty good nose then. Right?"

They were standing eye to eye. Then Tenisons laughed and waved his hand dismissively.

"*Bon voyage*, neighbour. *Cuba si, yankee no!*"[7]

---

7   "Cuba yes, Yankee no!" (Spanish) A popular Castro regime slogan at that time (author's note).

17

"So, he didn't come after all…"

He was startled out of his thoughts. Tenisons and Marika were already a distance away.

"He didn't come."

He'd forgotten about Aparjods. Aparjods was sitting on the bench and kicking at the rocks on the ground.

"That's life. Some come, some don't."

"Nobody came for you either?"

"For me?" A twinge of bitterness ran through Aparjods's voice. "Why would you think that I was waiting for anybody? This was just a simple misunderstanding. And misunderstandings are cleared up."

"Forgive me. I'll go."

"Where to?"

"The hospital."

"You don't need to go anywhere. I'll take you."

"Thank you, but it's not far."

"Near or far, it doesn't matter."

He wanted to get away as soon as he could and be by himself. Even if only for a few minutes. The most important thing right now was to carefully evaluate everything. There was no sense in lingering any longer with Aparjods.

"Thank you, I'll walk."

"Don't talk nonsense. That would be idiotic. I have to drive by the hospital anyway."

Aparjods walked out on to the road and waved to the taxi; it was parked and its "Reserved" sign was turned on. It was clearly waiting. The driver was the same one who had taken him to the mortuary earlier.

"To the hospital," Aparjods said, sitting down in the front seat.

"Hopefully, I won't need to wait there too," the driver said.

"I'll decide that. Now drive!"

"I waited for twenty-two minutes."

"That's the nature of your job."

"I can't work like that."

"Don't talk, just drive where I tell you to drive."

He shouldn't have gotten in. Why did he get in? Clearly, it was as hopeless trying to argue with Aparjods as it was trying to move the Powder Tower.[8] Luckily, the hospital wasn't far.

They had already driven across the bridge; the car rattled and creaked as it raced up the hill.

"Stop! Halt!"

The driver didn't want to stop on the slope and only pressed the brakes once he'd made it into the square, across from the monument. Aparjods immediately shoved open the door and got out. Gatiņš was shuffling vigorously towards them from the direction of the bridge with an umbrella under his arm and packet of books in his hand.

"Get in!"

It seemed like Gatiņš hadn't recognised Aparjods from a distance. He wasn't paying any attention to his shouting, but his ears pricked up as he got closer.

"Ah! It's the two of you!"

He didn't dawdle much and quickly got in, pushing his possessions ahead of him.

"You said you were going fishing," Aparjods said shooting a sideways glance at Gatiņš's pack of books.

"Something more urgent came up. A little old lady's house is being torn down tomorrow. I went through the things in her attic."

"Also fishing of a sort. How did it go?"

"I can't complain: seven Häcker Vidzeme Calendars beginning with 1851."[9]

"A measly, pitiful catch. If you're fishing for calendars, then

---

8   *Pulvertornis*, or the Powder Tower, is a well-known landmark in the Old Town district of the Latvian capital, Riga.

9   Häcker Vidzeme Calendars: one of the first periodicals published in Latvian, the Vidzeme Calendar was published annually and, in addition to a traditional calendar, included articles on religion and other topics (author's note).

that's no catch at all. I have the Vidzeme Calendar from 1792 published in Ķieģeļmuiža by Reverend Harder of Rubene knocking around somewhere in my attic."

"No chance at all it's from ninety-two. As is general knowledge, Harder published the Vidzeme Calendar in Ķieģeļmuiža only until 1790. From 1792 until 1810 it was published by Müller in Riga."

"That's an entirely different calendar. It was compiled by von Bergmann and later on by Ageluth. But I have the calendar published by Harder in Ķieģeļmuiža in 1792. Would you like to place a wager? For seven bottles of cognac – either ours or French, whichever is to your liking. Just not anything from Yugoslavia and definitely nothing from Romania; my stomach hurts the next morning after drinking it."

The taxi stopped in front of the hospital. He thanked Aparjods and got out. In the heat of their argument, the professor looked back indifferently and made a dismissive motion with his hand.

He was happy to be rid of Aparjods and Gatiņš, but his heart didn't lighten with his mood. Every step towards the hospital doors felt heavy, as if he were attached to the yoke in Ilya Repin's *Barge Haulers on the Volga*. There wasn't time to change any of his plans or come up with new ones. He had to go inside. Of course, he could still wait until the taxi left and then stroll a bit around the greenery in front of the hospital or down one of the streets nearby. But actually, better to go in right away. Then it would be done and over with.

He knew the way to the surgery area. But he felt like a thief or an insolent pest. Someone who had broken into an area where he didn't have the remotest right to be: any second now, he'd be seen and stopped, they'd ask for an explanation, berate him, and then kick him out. Luckily there was a fairly large number of people in the corridor. He wasn't noticed. The desk of the nurse on duty was obscured by young men crowding around to see the football game on the television.

A narcissist. A colossal narcissist. He always thought

only about himself. Only himself. Even when Lība's life was flickering like a candle in the wind. The same with his love for his father – just narcissism. His father – he'd been his Great Wall of China, his greenhouse, his easy life, and the fulfilment of his every wish. It wasn't hard to love his father. But what had he given in return? How had he helped his father during his hard times, what did he even know of his father's worries and misfortunes? Those didn't concern him. It was probably for that same reason that he never "clicked" with his mother. And what if she'd been very unhappy? He'd only cared about his rights, not his responsibilities. Easy and convenient…

The handle rattled too loudly. A nurse was standing with her back to the door in the middle of the hallway studying a small ampoule she had lifted up to the light. Hearing the noise, she turned her head.

"Where are you going? Visiting hours are over."

He couldn't sense any emotion in her eyes, which were the colour of forget-me-nots, or in the hushed, reserved tone of her voice. She was sterile, sharp, and cold. One look was enough to understand that trying to awaken any sense of compassion in her was utterly hopeless.

"I came to see if there was news on Lība Marcinkēviča. The doctor mentioned earlier that I should come by a bit later."

"I don't know. Without the doctor's permission…"

"Where could I find the doctor?"

"The doctor is occupied right now in the operating room."

"Thank you. I'm sorry. But maybe you could tell me. Is she doing any better?"

"I can't say. She's sleeping. Sleep always comes after surgery."

"Maybe she needs something, you see, she doesn't have anybody here."

"It doesn't seem that way to me. You're at least the fifth person to come in the past hour."

"Impossible."

"I know how to count to five. The last two people were here a few minutes before you."

The nurse put the ampoule in her pocket and slowly approached him, which could mean only one thing – a clear signal for him to leave.

A little further on, an elderly caretaker wobbled past him carrying a covered enamel dish. He stepped quickly to the side.

"I just wanted to ask…"

"It's completely impossible without the doctor's permission. Everybody has to follow the rules, that includes you and me."

"Certainly. But maybe you could make an exception just this once: I wanted to see where she's sleeping. My train leaves in an hour."

"What does that have to do with the hospital rules? If everybody only did what they wanted…"

"Even if just through a crack in the door…"

"Please leave. You're disturbing my work."

"No."

"What do you mean, 'no'?"

"I have to see her. I can't leave like this. I'll wait for the doctor."

"You're welcome to, but behind the doors leading to this section."

"Just let me look. And I'll disappear right away. On the spot."

"I'm calling the security guard."

"You'll be needlessly troubling him."

"You think that everything has to happen just like you want it to?"

"That would be the least of it. I fear I'm even a bit worse than that. Please!"

The nurse was standing motionless in front of him – her body was short, straight, her neck erect. He couldn't pinpoint the exact moment it happened, but suddenly he saw that this cold, hard face had changed. Like a lead button on a red-hot pan. Her face remained hard and emotionless, but she clearly cared, because she gave in and allowed him to see Lība.

"Come with me," she said, "but only for a moment."

She walked without looking back, with quick, quiet steps; he stepped carefully and struggled to keep up.

It was the last room at the end of the hallway, next to a window facing a brick wall. He didn't know why he'd hoped Lĭba would be alone in her room, but there were two beds. The one that was closer to the door was concealed by a folding screen. Everything past the end of the screen though was visible: at first it seemed like the bed was empty, the blanket looked like it had been flattened out and it showed almost no rise. But a head was visible on the pillow – white hair and a pale yellow face – skin and bones.

Thank God, at least that wasn't Lĭba. The screen made him shiver.

Lĭba's bed was the exact opposite. It looked like it was piled high. She couldn't take up that much space herself. There was surely some kind of rack or other equipment. But her face looked flushed, as if she'd spent the entire day sunning herself at the riverside.

"Go ahead, you can get closer."

"No, no, thank you."

He stayed right there standing in the doorway. The nurse took Lĭba's hand and quietly stared at her watch.

He felt that he could also hear the mechanical pulse of the watch. It was shrill and cutting, like the creaking of rusty hinges, like cutting with a blunt saw. Somewhere outside two sparrows were fighting. Incoherent, muffled rattling erupted from the direction of the screen.

"It looks like she's doing better," he said once they were standing in the hallway again. "If the operation was a success…"

The nurse turned the ampoule in her fingers without answering.

"Everything is fine, isn't it?"

"One can never be sure."

Suddenly he felt his lips starting to shake and his gaze clouding over. He was terribly ashamed, but he couldn't control his tears. He hung his head and gritted his teeth, but the tears rolled down his cheeks and on to his neck

"Are you going to wait for the doctor?"

"No, no, thank you."

"Call or, best of all, come by tomorrow."

"Thank you. I'm so sorry. It all turned out so absurdly. I don't understand…"

"I understand."

"No, you don't understand. Nobody can understand."

"Well, be that as it may, rules are rules," said the nurse, "and the hospital is still a hospital. We need order."

The door slammed shut even more loudly than when he'd arrived. A draft – he thought. There's a window open somewhere.

That's it. End of story. Now he could go anywhere and do anything. He could leave. Sit a while on the bench next to the greenery. Get drunk. Anything.

He just had to move more slowly. Good God in the highest, why was he running? Because of pride. Because of shame. Was he really running away? And if he ended up running into that nurse again someday…

He'd be truly wicked if he comforted himself right now with the thought that he'd be out on the street again in just a moment. Though even as he confronted his own conscience he had to admit that he felt great relief getting out of that tiny room. And she was just sleeping. The old lady was also alive. Two beds and two people. But maybe that was actually the worst of it, that they were alive…

He wanted to feel concern for Liba, but couldn't help but feel happy that it wasn't him lying there. For the first time ever he felt life itself manifested purely physically, like a gust of wind in his face, like the blade of a knife. But was that life? Brr. He clearly remembered that chill, that pressing, piercing chill.

He shivered. There wasn't any sense in thinking about any of that any longer. In sports they'd say, His nerves got the better of him. His imagination was too rich and sometimes that interfered with his ability to simply live. Apparently, he needed to approach everything more practically: things just are a certain way. After all, there wasn't anything he could change or fix. Could it be that he'd exaggerated his part in these events just a little bit? He knew so little about Lība. Honestly, they were practically strangers. They'd written letters to each other – big deal! And anyway – why did he even come here? Was that a help to somebody? Is anyone the better for it? What an idiot. A sensible person would never have done anything of the sort. If you do something, you must consider the consequences. But him? Wasn't he really a lot like Lība?

The taxi was waiting in front of the hospital. They hadn't left.

"Well? How is she?" Gatiņš asked.

He shrugged.

"Nothing's clear."

"That's a good sign. Women have a strong will to live. At moments like these, it's especially important whether the patient wants to live or not."

"Get in. Those who want to live don't jump out of windows," Aparjods growled.

"A fit of passion may last for only a moment, after that one's survival instinct reasserts itself. Did you speak with her?"

"No, she was sleeping."

"Conscious?"

"I think so."

"Then everything will be fine."

"Optimism also belongs to characteristics associated with 'good people'," Aparjods said.

"Optimism is a part of one's survival instinct."

"But there's the problem – part of one's instinct, not their reason. Nature hasn't entrusted any great importance to human reason."

"The professor and I ended up having a bit of an argument

while we were waiting," Gatiņš smiled guiltily. "How does it seem to you, is man good or evil by nature?"

"I haven't thought about it."

"But how does it seem to you?"

"Good and evil."

"Exactly: good and evil," Aparjods said these words while shaking his index finger. "But some want to turn man into an angel and then wonder why his wings won't stay put."

"To claim that man does not improve is to deny evolution."

"To claim, to deny. Science isn't religion. Give me facts. Earth has existed long enough in that case to have turned into paradise long ago. Maybe you also think that black folk will eventually turn white?"

"That's not what I was saying. It may be that in time white folk will turn black. Black folk are more fertile."

"Well, that would be fine then," Aparjods said, "let's stop by the all-night delicatessen."

"Where?"

"Everything has already been decided. You just have to raise your hand and say 'yes'. Gatiņš has a sauna. It turns out there's also a sauna at that manor house of his. How many hours for it to be ready?"

"With our modern technology it's fast. One sneeze and it'll be ready."

"Is there anything better than a country sauna? Young man, don't hang your head, we'll be whistling with delight in that sauna."

"You can't whistle in a sauna. Whoever whistles in a sauna summons the devil…"

"If only all those who we summoned always responded…"

"The commandments of the religion of the sauna are strict: whoever pisses in the sauna will have sweaty hands; whoever kills a flea in the sauna will have terrible luck; whoever leaves water in the buckets will lose their voice. After washing, everyone has to stand up and pour water over themselves saying, 'Water going down as I get up!'"

He didn't care. It was possible that it was better to be in the company of Aparjods and Gatiņš. The loud words washing back and forth relaxed him, much like the pitter-patter of rain on the roof or the splashing of waves against the side of a boat. At least he wouldn't be forced by his thinking to denigrate himself.

"Gatiņš, tell me honestly for once, what do you think, does God exist?"

"God might not exist, but the devil definitely does."

Aparjods got out at the delicatessen and after a short while was standing in the doorway and beckoning.

"Boys, come grab the case of beer! Driver, open the trunk!"

Aparjods was holding all manner of packages and tins in his hands.

Gatiņš gripped his head with both hands, startled.

"Where do you want to put all of that?"

"Just stay calm. For Latvians no entertainment is complete if at the end of it they haven't had the chance to stuff themselves full. What else do we need? Green soap?"

"There's soap already."

"Then let's go."

"We're off!"

The driver no longer looked disgruntled, but instead was smiling and satisfied.

They raced through the town. The streams of drivers and pedestrians had thinned. Cars decorated with now wilting birch branches returned from who knows where bringing back tired day trippers. Wives were taking home their husbands and sleeping children. Lively groups of young people stood on street corners saying their goodbyes and going their separate ways.

In the daylight, the large trees in the park looked fairly normal; the excavated street was covered in dust. The bypass went along the edge of a sickly fallow and an old stone barn. This probably had been the centre of a manor. But further on the road began again with its family homes flanked by gardens.

"Look, there's smoke coming out of the sauna chimney! Velta is already warming it up," Gatiņš pointed.

"What – does she know?"

"One develops the ability to sense such things when married."

In the yard, standing against the gate, was a red Java.[10] As he walked by, Gatiņš pressed the horn, but jumped away startled at the sound of its piercing shriek.

"Do you own a motorcycle?"

"No, I don't think so."

Loud voices shot towards them from the direction of the garden. Aparjods turned his head attentively.

"What's happening over there? It smells like sausages."

"No idea."

He saw Tenisons first. Jubilant, overcome by the joy of victory, so delighted he was smiling like an idiot. The owner of the motorcycle was standing next to him dressed in a black leather jacket. Just look!

"...the lord of the manor home at last, hooray, exactly as if we'd agreed, it must be fate... Marika get the glasses, let's drink to a lucky meeting... the sauna is already warming up, I didn't know what to do... where were you after you left the house in the morning..."

Tenisons's laughter, which followed, cut through the noise.

Marika was sitting on a blanket on the grass. The woman next to her, who was young and somewhat plump already, was probably Gatiņš's wife Velta. Gatiņš couldn't keep his glasses on his nose again: they were constantly sliding down despite being vigorously pushed back up. Aparjods, pointing at the case of beer, was saying something to him, and Gatiņš shrugged and rubbed his chin before finally taking Aparjods over to Velta.

"Hey! Wimp, you old rat, do you see that guy over there..." The motorcyclist shoved Tenisons and pointed his finger through the crowd directly at him.

---

10   Java: a Czech motorcycle company popular at that time (author's note).

167

"I'll introduce you right away."

"Thanks, that's alright, we already know each other."

That was a blow for Tenisons. He hadn't been expecting that.

"Since when?"

"Since we were kids, my friend, since we were kids."

"You're putting me on."

"You think it's a joke? Cain murdered Abel because of jokes like that."

"So you probably haven't seen each other in a long time?"

"Sure. In three days it'll be a week."

The motorcyclist was already standing right in front of him and the sound of him punching at his shoulder echoed with a loud pop. He put his arm around him and held him in a steel embrace. He shoved him, jostled him, drove his fist into the pit of his stomach. Tenisons didn't take a single step back.

"What are you doing here, buddy?"

"Nothing. I'm just here."

"You're lying, you old devil. You won't put one over on me. I've got a sixth sense when it comes to stuff like this. You're not just anybody. But somehow I thought you were weak."

You couldn't expect him to be especially refined. He always said what was in his heart.

"But what are you doing here?"

"Was passing by, just stopped for a visit. See, it turns out this toady here, Wimp, is a relative of mine. Mother's brother's cousin twice removed or something like that."

"Sure..."

"Nothing strange about it, like they say: we choose our friends, but God chooses our family for us."

"Sometimes relatives bring huge surprises with them." Tenisons closed his left eye pensively, as if he were aiming a pool cue.

"Calm down, you old rat, we don't see each other that much."

Now it was clear why Tenisons had hoped to keep him

around "at least until Sunday night"! Something was going to happen any second now, there was no doubt about it. Tenisons had been patient and had been waiting for too long to relent now. He'd been hoping for a scandal. He was craving it. He needed it. Apparently, as a kind of payback, because of the letters addressed to Marika.

It turned out there weren't enough glasses, so Velta ran inside. Gatiņš was opening beer bottles by knocking off their caps against the edge of the case. The noise of the crowd when they first arrived was replaced by tense activity, with conversation unsteadily switching from one topic to the next.

"...yes, crayfish boiled with dill would really be perfect right now... Gatiņš, go and see if the sauna is ready... there are so many mosquitoes this year, are there mosquitoes in Riga too? Why is Velta going to so much trouble, you can drink beer from a bottle, back in my grandfather's day nobody had glasses, everyone drank from the same mug..."

"Listen, I'm jumping on my bike in a second and riding off, I can't stand it, you're drinking beer, but I have to keep staring at it. What am I, some kind of a Baptist?"

"Abstinence builds character."

"To hell with abstinence! Is beer even an alcoholic drink? If it is, then Pertussin is alcohol too."

"Nobody knows how to drink beer any more. What kind of beer-drinking is that? Always in a rush, always in a rush, just to get it inside faster. Beer drinking is an extended process. Treimanis-Zvārgulis worked as a clerk at the district court and lived there too, right up in the attic. Every Saturday night he'd go down to the Vērmaņdārzs restaurant and bring up two baskets of Bayerisch, and then anybody who wanted to could go and drink until Sunday night. Now that was beer drinking, that's something I can understand!"

Velta returned.

"Well, now that's not right at all either," Aparjods's angry face softened noticeably, "the lady of the house has an empty glass. My dear lady, allow me to propose a toast."

"To Velta, Jānis's daughter. And a lovely Saturday night!"

"Today is Sunday."

"Forgive me, sauna nights are always Saturday nights, independent of…"

"Quite right, a Soviet person goes to the sauna whenever he likes."

"Perhaps you'll allow me to also say a few words." Tenisons gave everyone there an insincerely enthusiastic look as he clutched his glass with white knuckles. The artificially friendly voice sounded gruff, tinged by a barely disguised chill. "A toast to the lady of the house is admirable and to the sauna – healthy. Things are as they are. That's difficult to deny. But I think we'd just be uncivilised if we didn't toast the guests tonight. I'd like to take advantage of the accidental luck or lucky accident, regardless of how everyone wants to see it, that we have several living legends in our midst, which doesn't happen too often for us out here in the provinces…"

"Wait, wait, I don't understand, what are we toasting?"

"Let's drink to the honourable old master, Professor Roberts Aparjods, and the young, talented poet, Aleksandrs Draiska…"

His intuition turned out to be right. A devilishly clever move… It'll be interesting to see what happens next, he thought, almost dispassionately as if it didn't even apply to him, but to somebody else instead.

Their gazes met for just an instant, and the air seemed to grow thick with confusion. The first one to come around was the motorcyclist, who pushed Tenisons aside and toasted very formally first with Aparjods and then with him.

"To your health, comrade professor! To your health, young poet!"

Tenisons was paying attention so closely that he was hunched forward. He wasn't smiling any more, but watching with tense curiosity. It was as if he'd lit a sparkler by the holiday tree with clear foreknowledge of what would happen, and was now only waiting until his hopes were fulfilled. He hadn't foreseen what had happened and it had surprised him greatly.

Finally sensing something, he grabbed the motorcyclist by the elbow, causing some of his beer to slosh out of his glass.

"Aleksandrs, don't fool around! This is no time for games."

The motorcyclist turned abruptly and with a single sharp movement freed himself from Tenisons's grasp.

"My thoughts exactly."

"This isn't any kind of a joke…"

"Then don't joke around. And spill beer. Of course, my dear relative! You have to know how to behave in public."

"Are you telling me he is Aleksandrs Draiska? If so, many apologies, but then who are you!"

"No sense carrying on any longer. His name is Kaspars Krūmiņš."

"It's clear as day, they've found something to argue about," Aparjods growled. "I thought people start to lose their minds only when they get old, but it turns out that this affliction also hobbles the young."

"His name is Kaspars Krūmiņš!"

"That doesn't necessarily mean anything," Gatiņš shrugged his shoulders. "Rainis's name was Pliekšāns and Stalin was actually Jugashvili."[11]

Velta apparently didn't understand the reason for the argument – maybe it was serious, maybe it was a joke, but she didn't like its combative tone.

"Listen all of you, why are you doing this? In such nice weather, on such a nice evening… Be sensible. Just like card players, as soon as you're together you have to start arguing."

"Madam, there is nothing to be upset about. Arguments are normal. As long as man has existed, arguments have also existed. Independent of meteorological conditions."

"Velta, wait," a flushed Marika rebuked her sister, "don't get involved. I can't take it any longer. We should say once and for all who each of us really is."

---

11 *Jānis Rainis* (born Jānis Pliekšāns): one of the most prominent figures in Latvian literature, known for his work as a poet and playwright.

"As if anybody knows that," the professor added. "And in any case, show me anyone who actually wants to be who they are. The tall dream of being short, the short of being tall. Scoundrels wish they had honour, while those with honour despair at not being clever enough."

"This matter is much too serious," Tenisons wasn't giving up.

"Please don't exaggerate, my dear relative. Yesterday in Riga, for example, I met two other people named Tenisons."

"Did you?"

"Yes. And they passed along their greetings to you. I think you wanted to drink to the poet's health. Best not to draw that out. The poet, as far as I know, is in a hurry."

"What do you mean? Did you want to leave?"

"Yes, let's both get on the road."

"Really?"

Another astonishing move by Aleksandrs. He had to focus on controlling himself so that his affirmative answer didn't sound too eager.

"Yes."

Gatiņš furrowed his brow.

"Right now when the sauna is ready? Are you crazy? Don't be foolish."

"No other way. There's a long trip ahead."

Velta also tried to object, but it seemed more out of politeness.

"Well, then at least finish your beer."

Tenisons and Gatiņš walked with them to the gate. The former, still convinced he had been right, was angry and offended but tried to seem cool and reserved.

"I didn't know you were working together," Tenisons said smiling thinly as he bade goodbye to Aleksandrs.

"No worries, old man, no worries, it'll be fine. Making mistakes is human. I really despise public scandals."

"And I really despise lies. One should never think too little of others and too much of oneself. I just don't understand…"

"…I also don't understand many things. Your wife Anita, for

example, was telling me yesterday about changing flats, about moving to be with you in Randava, about kindergarten…"

Tenisons's entire body slumped.

"No sense talking about it here, it's a serious and complicated thing. We're getting divorced, but it doesn't happen that quickly."

"So it seems."

"Right now I don't have time to deal with a court case."

"That's what you tell Marika."

"Thanks…"

"So, Saint Anthony, best not to get too high and mighty."

"I still think you're leaving unforgivably early." Gatiņš walked up and gripped his hand. "It was very nice to meet you and to speak with you. Believe me, a person without a secret is like a nail pulled from its board. A very dull business."

"Whatever," Tenisons waved his hand dismissively.

"Bon voyage." Gatiņš's glasses slipped down his nose again. "And never forget what Michelangelo Buonarroti wrote to one of his brothers in 1515, though which one has not yet been determined: 'Sleep with your eyes open, you must always be aware of your body and soul.'"

18

The Java lurched forward like it had been thrown from a catapult and then, puttering quietly, raced ahead. It seemed like its tyres didn't even touch the ground. Only in the town centre at intersections did its flight occasionally pause, the rhythm of its motor coming to an abrupt halt and its springs gently vibrating.

It felt like the two of them were moving through a dense, whistling wall of air. Every once in a while, Aleksandrs would glance back over his shoulder and flash him a faunlike smile with his wide mouth full of teeth.

"Hold on! It'll be quicker on the highway!"

They crossed the bridge and Aleksandrs yelled, "We have to stop for petrol!"

A longish line of vehicles stretched behind the petrol pump.

"Well, click your heels together and tell your uncle thanks. Didn't I pull you out of a tight spot yet again? I'd almost forgotten what was up. That Varis is a real piece of work. It ended up being a real hassle for me."

"Terrible stuff."

"Of course, you can understand him a bit. Offended, jealous, and so on. That's when all kinds of feelings can bubble up. Apparently, he's unhappy that Marika was involved. His lady-love is compromised."

"It all ended up such a stupid mess."

"I heard. Please accept my condolences."

"If I'd only known back then…"

Aleksandrs looked at him with surprise and said, chortling loudly, "Listen, my friend, honestly, it's not nothing to get agitated about… Don't let it get to you. That's exactly why it's interesting, because you couldn't have predicted any of it. It's a game."

"But she's lying in the hospital."

"Well, she's completely deranged. A fool or a psychopath. In this enlightened and pragmatic century of ours. Grandmother told me once about the unfortunate Baroness Doroteja, who jumped out of a window because at her first ball her nerves caused her to emit a rude noise. At least you can still understand that somewhat: the traditions of the time, aristocratic narrow-mindedness, crinolines, corsets, and liquid ammonia. It even has its own sort of drama. But today!"

"It's possible that it wasn't even on purpose. And it's not important anyhow. She was completely dismayed."

"They're awfully sly. And with all sorts of problems. I had a lady, before my military service, who descended upon me like a curse, called on the phone, wrote letters. Then once in a moment of weakness I thought, Well, I'll go over there, it's not a problem. But listen, she didn't let me in, said, 'It's late already, there's nobody here, we don't know each other well enough.'"

It was pointless to talk to him. He understood nothing. Each of them was talking about something else.

Aleksandrs pushed the motorcycle closer to the gas pump, lifted it up on to its support, and stretched his arms; his muscles moved like iron pistons in his black leather sleeves.

"You know, I've had just about enough. Going back to old pastures like this is just too hard. I think I need to put on the brakes."

"Are you spending time in Riga?"

"That would be making too much of a generalisation. I work in more intimate surroundings."

"Have you already submitted your papers to the university?"

"First I'd like to get a good night's sleep."

He pushed his hand into his coat pocket and took out a photograph cut into the shape of an oval.

"Look at this, my friend, what a girl. Have you ever seen anything like that? World class. A European exterior combined with an Asian temperament. One of a kind. In any genre, including romance, you need a special hook – God-given gifts."

Maybe his mood was the cause, but he was overcome by a biting, loathsome sense of apathy. He hung his head so he wouldn't have to look Aleksandrs in the eyes. This face, he knew it down to the tiniest detail, a face that he'd seen day in and day out for three years, waking up in the morning and going to sleep at night, always to his left in formation, right across from him at the table, under a steel helmet on the training field, breathing heavily behind the fogged-up goggles of his gas mask, sweaty in the showers and standing still in the freezing cold, with a blackish, freshly shaved, uneven neck and short, messy hair – suddenly, this face seemed incredibly disgusting to him. In fact, this feeling somehow stretched back into the past. As if he'd also found it disgusting long ago, but had only come to realise it now.

Aleksandrs had wound himself up and continued to brag in his usual way, astonishingly satisfied with himself as well as being self-assured, loud and childishly naive. He understood nothing at all. Nothing at all. Though he was supposedly a decent guy. Bright even. Brave, reliable, talented. Why had he been so taken with Aleksandrs all these years, and had envied him and even tried to imitate him?

While he was talking, Aleksandrs worked deftly with the mixing vessel, and the oil and gas mixture flowed into the tank with a gurgling sound.

"All set! Now you'll get to see what happens if you rub some turpentine under the devil's tail. Time it."

Aleksandrs clipped the strap of the red plastic helmet underneath his chin and pushed the transparent visor down across his face.

"Saddle up!"

The cobblestones on the road leading to the highway clattered under their wheels again. A cold wind began whistling past his ears. Houses, trees, telephone poles whizzed past. Biruta's and Caune's familiar faces appeared for just a second within this swaying, ever more distorted kaleidoscope of flowing colours and forms. They were standing on the side of the road or perhaps going somewhere. It was just one moment and then they disappeared. But it was enough for him.

"Wait! Stop!" He grabbed Aleksandrs's shoulder sharply. The Java reared up like a horse stopped in mid-gallop.

"Hey, hey, what's up?"

"I'm not going."

"You afraid?"

He looked back. Biruta and Caune were standing on the edge of the road looking towards him.

"Oh, so that's how things are! Well, whatever you want. Your business," Aleksandrs let out a long roaring laugh, "it doesn't matter to me."

"I have to talk to them… Don't wait for me!"

"As you wish."

This time Aleskandrs's voice sounded different somehow. Maybe he understood after all and was just playing along, staying true to his style. He gunned the engine and left, disappearing into the distance along with the sound of his motor.

He shoved his wind-ruffled shirt deeper into his trousers, straightened his coat, and crossed the street. In the meantime, Biruta and Caune had turned around and were practically running away.

That's the only way it could've been, what else could he expect after everything that had happened. No, truly. It was logical and understandable. Still, there was a hint of bitterness in his heart: what fools they were, to kick up and run away, as if he were going to eat them.

"Biruta!"

The fleeing pair fell out of step and seemed to lose their resolve a bit. Biruta wanted to stop, but Caune tugged at her arm and tried pulling her forward.

"Please, wait! I need to tell you something…"

Heads down, they rushed even faster, despite him having almost caught up with them.

"Just a few words!"

Biruta looked back and slowed her pace. A struggle ensued again, but this time they stopped.

"Biruta, don't be a traitor... If you say even one word to him..."

"Of course. You think I'm a monster."

"Yes, exactly, the worst kind of monster."

"And it's all my fault alone?"

"It is your fault. It's a fact. Let's go, Biruta. Do you hear?"

"Well, wait a second, Džuljeta, you're exaggerating."

"Shame on you! If you speak to him..."

Caune tried shifting Biruta one more time, but convincing herself that it wasn't possible, angrily shoved away her friend's hand.

"Do what you like, I'm not going to argue with you. Go ahead and stay! Just without me. And don't forget that he hunts geese just like you."

She'd turned completely red from stress and anger, and ran away sniffling, barely keeping her tears back.

Biruta stood with her head down and avoided his gaze.

"And you also think I'm a monster?"

She turned towards him. But only with her eyes.

"No."

"Then maybe you don't know..."

"I know."

"What do you know?"

"At least half of it..."

They walked away from the town. Only occasionally did someone walk towards them.

"I spent the night next to Lība," Biruta added after a while. "If I'd had only the slightest sense..."

Biruta took out a handkerchief and blew her nose.

"It should've been clear. Nothing good was going to come of any of this."

"Why do you think that?"

"Because of what she told me. And knowing Lība... Life has never been easy for her."

"Do you believe in destiny?"

"I don't know what to believe in. I only know that always and through everything, a person needs luck on their side."

"We were taught in school that everyone is the master of their own fate."

"But one person crashes in a plane and survives, while another falls off a stool and is killed."

"But is it really right to blame only misfortune? At least this time, there are also other factors."

"No doubt. But everything has turned out badly for Lība since childhood. And she's used to that, in fact, she prepares herself for misfortune ahead of time."

"From her letters it seemed like she was carefree and happy."

"Then you don't really know her at all. I've read a lot about people like that. Their lack of confidence and initiative is a hidden trauma, not a feature of their personality. By their nature they're industrious and energetic, but at some point their outward initiative always dwindles and breaks down; this process builds up like a tormenting, contradictory force. Think about it: home is at the cemetery, right next to it is the chapel, funerals all the time, crying women, open caskets, the peal of bells, mourning songs. Do you think that doesn't have an effect? And do you know what they called her at school?"

"Yes, the Corpse Queen, her mother told me."

"It all seems very clear to me: a small, shy, introverted girl who gets ridiculed; she begins to be ashamed of her home, her mother, herself. Intellectually, she might understand that that's wrong, but not everything is determined by the intellect. You probably also know how it all ended?"

"Yes, Lība left home."

"And everything was fine again. She did well in school, she was elected head of her class. If she had gotten into the institute... But, as usual, it didn't work out for her. She had to gather up her documents and go home. That wouldn't be a happy time for anybody, but imagine how it was for Lība, she has so little self-confidence and so little belief in her own abilities. I remembered how we met for the first time. 'You forgot your coat,' I said to her, but she just looked at me wide-eyed without saying anything. She'd never thought she'd work in a factory. She was willing to work anywhere though, just so she didn't have to return home. She didn't like her job in the weaving mill, but she didn't have the courage or initiative to change things and start over again. Also, she was too proud to show her lack of ability to anybody else, she was afraid of pity.

"That's normal, people have a much easier time accepting their own weaknesses than having them discovered by others. She was looking for a place to hide and so played the part of 'the crazy one'. She thought that was an escape. And to exaggerate everything was in her nature. That's how the story about her time in prison came about. Stupid, isn't it? But still fundamentally understandable. And all of us were so naive and believed it. Though I suspect she became so comfortable playing that part that she started to believe it herself sometimes. Everybody noticed 'Crazy Liba', they laughed about her, but also were amazed by her, or at least just shrugged their shoulders – look, what a rare bird. That was fairly interesting and to a certain extent even romantic."

"I just don't understand why she had to come up with the story about the child."

"Why? Very simple. Guys came to see the girls in the dormitory, had parties. Of course, they'd invite Liba too. Last night she confessed to me: 'I was terrified, because I didn't know what to do, I thought they'd find me out at any moment. I'm an incredible fool,' she said, 'having lived all this time like in a dream. In high school at bedtime I'd say the same prayer every night:

"'Love, I call to you wherever I go!
When your brightness to a child of this earth is given,
He awakes forever young with his darkness riven.

"'And suddenly they'd be trying to kiss me with their stinking mouths. I thought,' she said, 'if one of them touches me, I'll die. In my mind I could already hear how they'd ridicule me for my virginity, they'd call me a nun and all sealed up. I was terribly afraid. And then I started to say I had a child and already had ten affairs in my past, that I'm one of those... well, one of those,' she said, even though she didn't even really know how children are made, yes, that's what she said, and only knew as much about love as is written in books and shown in the movies.

"You're not even listening. Lība told me all that last night. I thought I'd just go in and sleep in her room, as all the other girls had left. She was sitting at the desk and looked confused, staring at a single point with tears streaming endlessly down her face. You think Maṇa ironed your suit? It was Lība."

"I got her letter, but..."

"She wanted you to leave so badly; the note was all she could think to do in the short time she had."

"I'd have left if..."

"...if Kamita hadn't gotten involved."

"You can't blame Kamita for anything."

"Oh, but I think you can. She knew Lība wrote those letters. Or at least sensed it. At the very least she knew that the one you were looking for wasn't her.

"Of course, you can understand Kamita, getting married is the main thing for her; she'd decided that she'd definitely get married by autumn. But Lība wasn't thinking about that. The imaginary Lība lived, met with people, walked the town's streets, bragged and laughed, but the real Lība was hiding, alone, tormented by her failings – she was in agony.

"And then she read the poems in the magazine. And she thought there was something very familiar in them, as if those words, before being arranged into a poem, had come from her own self. I don't know how it is for you, but I know that feeling well. And she decided to write a letter, just to open her heart, to at least be honest for once. In case the letter was returned and some curious person had opened it – for some reason she kept thinking that the letter would be returned – she signed it using Marika's name. With no evil intent. Well, how can I explain it: by signing it 'Marika', Lība wasn't hiding anything. That was her, but behind an idealised mask. Or to say it even better, the way she had wanted to be.

"That's also the reason she sent Marika's photograph later on. She wanted to look like that. Her own photographs seemed too ordinary, too unimpressive. She was afraid that if you received one like that, you wouldn't write any more, and getting your letters had already become very important to her. Maybe she wanted to make you happy and thought you'd be happier getting a picture of Marika. I mean, I don't really know all the details either. Back then, of course, it never occurred to her that someday you might meet. And that was her problem, because to return to the truth later on is difficult. What good could come of it?"

"If only you'd told me all of that yesterday."

"I didn't even know all of it yesterday. Lība told it to me during the night."

"Yes. Then it was probably already too late."

"Too late."

"Too late…"

"It's probably hard for you to understand this. Honestly, I don't really understand either how a person can at once be who they are and who they aren't…"

"No," he said, looking into the distance where the frozen roadside trees were rising up dark and eerie against the bright night sky of the summer months, "I understand it. I understand it very well."

As they stood under the weight of the heavy silence, all of a sudden a black bat shot over them. He had to speak, he wanted to speak, that's exactly why he'd called out to Biruta and now she was standing next to him; he had to at least tell Biruta about it, at least her. But the silence was already moving down over their heads, filling their eyes and pressing their mouths shut, and so not a single word ended up being said.

19

No light was on in any of the windows, everyone was already asleep. Just haunting walls with prop roofs. Decorations. Emptiness, silence, and loneliness, the show was over, but the stage had been left as it was. A small safety light was glowing at the end of a pole. This might be Priežu Street. What did he need here, what was he looking for?

Along the edge of the fence it smelt of stock and gillyflower. The light bulb lit up the pale green leaves. And yet the stillness that surrounded him was just an illusion, there were other people somewhere nearby. Interesting, what would happen if he suddenly started to yell loudly – would lights turn on and windows open?

There was music in the distance. It sounded choppy and strange. These sounds too seemed familiar. The river had to be here just on the right. A tall, uniform fence rose up on the other side of the street. Old trees, alders and larches stretched across the top of the fence like a dark wall.

Some time later the street was flooded with a ghostly throng: the sound of their chatter grew louder as did the chaotic clatter of their footsteps, and he could hear stifled laughter and the rustle of their clothing and their movement. An event had ended at the stadium park. As they approached in the dark, he couldn't discern their faces, even their bodies seemed to flow together, at times resembling a giant multicoloured herd of grazing animals, rushing ahead and enveloped in a dust cloud that had spread out across the entire street, and at times like a column of soldiers marching in lockstep, tired yet full of strength, scattering yet still unified. The young women had the young men's coats draped over their shoulders. White shirts with rolled-up sleeves. Pale-coloured dresses on the women. Whistling, calls, songs stopping and starting, jokes, fragments of conversations, arguments.

The noisy crowd disappeared as unexpectedly as it had

appeared, amongst the stragglers a few affectionate couples were holding each other tightly and a group of local Beatles with guitars hanging around their shoulders slipped slowly by. He was once again surrounded by emptiness and silence.

What would he have told Lĩba if she'd opened her eyes earlier and could have listened to him? Empty phrases. Wishing her a speedy recovery. What a great guy, what a decent man. Noble, innocent, forthright. All because, by coincidence, Lĩba knows less about him than he does about Lĩba.

The path led up the hill. There were many steps, the warm wooden railing swayed and creaked mournfully. A narrow bridge stretched across the ravine. After it more steps. And then a tightly overgrown tree-lined path resembling a dark tube. After becoming accustomed to the light, his eyes discovered alcoves with benches and millstone tables. The square where the path ended seemed unusually bright. And the view extended far into the distance. Darkness lay below, but a clear, translucent, bluish sky glowed above him.

The old castle ruins were right there. He stood in a crumbling opening where a window had been. A rock, inadvertently disturbed by his foot, rolled over the edge of the wall and fell into the darkness. The sound of its impact only reached him after a longer moment. He pulled away instinctively. To fall into the darkness – that must be terrible. One fatal move and there's nothing to be done. In fact, the worst of it probably isn't even the impact but the fall, when the mind is working a thousand times its normal speed and sees everything from the perspective of the inevitable.

What did she think, what did she feel, before the impact came?

He forced himself to return to the window's edge and this time pushed down a fragment of plaster on purpose. His ears started to ring and a strange vacuum formed in his head. He supported himself against the wall surrounding the window opening and then ran off. Terrible! Why was he fooling around here? As if it were a joke.

There was absolutely nothing he could say to Lĩba. And

that's why he couldn't go to see her. He'd missed that moment long ago, let it pass him by. They couldn't meet again without feeling guilty. Everything was ruined. And there was nothing to be saved or changed. He had to make peace with that.

His presence at the hospital would serve no purpose. A sentimental gesture, a cool compress for his conscience, self-delusion, something to soothe his own nerves. That was the worst kind of weakness. He just lacked the strength to go, to admit that everything had been destroyed and ruined. To accept responsibility and guilt. He still just wanted something to hope for, something to anticipate. But there was no sense looking back any more.

The silence breathed with barely perceptible gusts of wind. There was the sound of footsteps somewhere in the distance, clipped voices and laughter. A woman's heels clicked rhythmically across the pavement.

"What are you doing tomorrow?"

"You mean today."

"Oh, of course, it's already two."

"Nothing. I'm going to sleep until lunchtime, I've got an evening shift."

The cobblestone road was brightly lit. A black cat, its tail sticking straight up, walked down the middle of the street. Light was streaming from the windows of a restaurant; the cleaners must have still been working there. Too bad. This would have been just the time to go up and get drunk. Today there was truly a reason.

A young man with dishevelled hair was sitting on the bench by the newspaper stand.

"Hey man, do you have any matches?" The youth shook as he yawned.

"No, I don't." For some reason he touched his pockets.

"What a dead end. Well, tell me – what are two maniacs like us good for?"

"We've got to go."

The young man scratched his hairy chest and let out a roar of a laugh. "We've got to go... we've got to go... Total genius. And so easy, right? You don't have any matches, but maybe a car?"

If he remembered correctly, a long-distance high-speed train was leaving for Riga closer to the morning.

The bridge. The café. The bus station. The gas pump. In the stillness of the night you could hear a locomotive raging – hissing and groaning as it tried to move the carriages, its wheels slipping, the rhythm of the steam it exhaled breaking up and stopping suddenly, transforming into hollow wheezing.

The red signal light twinkled at the end of the factory chimney. The dormitory's white brick structure seemed strangely abandoned. Lība had grown up at the cemetery. The cemetery always makes one feel unpleasantly anxious at night. A foolish hangover from the past. This quiet, white building also made the hair stand up on the back of his neck: he walked without taking his eyes off of the single light bulb lighting the doorway, not knowing what he was expecting, only that something was about to happen. But maybe it was much simpler, maybe he was just afraid of running into one of the girls. Kamita, for example. Lība couldn't come out, she was lying in that small room with the old, dying woman.

Fortunately, that was all in the past. Everything was in the past. Soon he'd be taking his seat on the train and in a few hours he'd be in Riga.

The loud knock of footfalls eroded the silence of the street. The bakery. The shoe shop. The "agritech" storage depot. Further on, the street had been excavated by sewage workers. It smelt of recently sawn wooden boards, one of his favourite smells. The station square, fringed by shadows, seemed unusually small. Old Mārtiņš's kvass barrel seemed to be floating along on top of the darkness.

At long last his hand shoved open the heavy station door, overcoming the noticeable resistance with practically a physical sense of delight. The ticket window was closed;

he knocked on the glass. A moment later a woman's head emerged from the bluish-yellow light.

"Will the train to Riga be arriving soon?"

"As scheduled."

"One ticket, please."

"Of course, but it's the fast train and costs three times more."

"I don't care."

He shoved the ticket into his pocket and suddenly felt unbelievably tired. The air in the station hall was warm and stale, thick like gelatine. If the clock was right, then the train had to be there soon. The rails glowed brilliant white in the moonlight.

Aside from him, there was only one other person waiting at the station. He shot him a quick glance and flinched, as if he'd seen an apparition. It was Professor Aparjods. But from where? Had he really been following him? Aparjods also looked over. They looked at each other for a long time. Aparjods was smoking.

"We're running into each other everywhere tonight."

"That would be hard to deny."

"Are you also going to Riga?"

"Are you going to Riga?"

"Yes."

"And you're in quite a rush?"

Was there ridicule hiding in Aparjods's words, a roundabout nod at his undignified escape?

"There's nothing left for me to do in Randava."

"As far as I remember, you were taking care of some business here."

"It's all taken care of."

"Congratulations."

A thin smile flashed across Aparjods's thick lips.

"I envy you. That must be a wonderful feeling when everything is taken care of."

Aparjods looked extremely strange. There was some kind

of crushing insecurity visible behind his usual stance and manner of speech. Had he had more to drink than usual or was he ill perhaps?

"You're also going to Riga?"

"No," Aparjods shook his head.

"Are you staying in Randava?"

"I, unfortunately, haven't taken care of all of my business yet. But there's not much time left. If you want to know – there's only very little time left…"

Even Aparjods's voice sounded strange – one could almost say sentimental, if the clipped words didn't also contain a hint of something antagonistic.

"Vilis and I were in the same year. Since the time we'd scurried off to school, since the time we came to Riga. In '29. That year it was an unusually late spring. The lilacs were still blooming on Peter Day.[12] We rented a furnished room on Mednieku Street on the sixth floor. From Mrs Hofmanis… I'd already forgotten about it, but the day before yesterday when I saw you, I suddenly remembered. Do you know when a person becomes old? When he's lost the courage to start all over again. That's probably the reason new generations of people keep being born. It's just like with paper money: worn, dirty or torn notes are taken out of circulation and replaced with new ones. The world is founded on the courage to start everything over again from the beginning. And on the belief that it really is a new beginning. If you have a son, then you can at least hope…"

The signal turned green. A train would be coming at any moment.

He looked off anxiously into the distance, searching for the

12 Peter Day is 29 June. Latvia, much as other countries in the region, has a tradition of celebrating "name days". A certain number of names is assigned to each day on the calendar and then each day is celebrated somewhat like a birthday with friends and family of the person whose name is on the calendar that day.

column of light from the locomotive's front projector, unsure of what was upsetting him more – his impatience to spot the train and be rid of Aparjods, or the fear that this conversation might come to an end.

Aparjods certainly looked very odd. And spoke very oddly. It was completely impossible to predict what this version of Aparjods would do or say in the next moment. It seemed like even Aparjods didn't really know. Something had happened to Aparjods. And just then the train approached. No, he wanted to hear what he had to say after all.

The point of light which had appeared in the distance was growing brighter.

Nonsense. It's none of his business. He was dead tired, his head as full as a toilet tank. He was beaten up and torn to pieces. And he didn't care about anything.

"No, I'm wrong," Aparjods said, "I don't envy you. You're the same kind of know-nothing that everybody is in their youth. And until you understand what's happening in the world, life will keep getting the best of you. But I do envy Vilis. Something will remain of him. Life is, in a sense, like homework at school: you have to complete the assignment and turn in your notebook. You should know that. At least you couldn't have forgotten that yet."

"I've forgotten a lot."

"That you have to turn in your notebook? Nonsense! You have to remember that. Everyone can make mistakes, but it's important that you notice them. Sometimes in the beginning it seems like you're doing well, you're proud and very satisfied with yourself. But then things start to catch and come apart and then it gradually becomes clear that it's all been ruined. But you don't believe it, you lack the courage to admit the truth. Instead you try to fool yourself with your own lies: everything is fine, nothing to worry about... But the truth always comes out anyway. And you still have to turn in your notebook. Nice, isn't it?"

"That can happen."

"And you know you're actually turning in an empty notebook. But it could have been another way…"

"Probably so."

"Why are you sighing? You've taken care of all your business… Your life is happiness and love – joy… You have real friends and at night you're tired. Oh, beautiful, new beginning!"

The train was clearly visible now, there was a slight curve in the rails by the switch. A long line of rail cars came into view.

"So, you're leaving?"

Instead of answering he quietly showed him his ticket.

Aparjods's heavy owl-like eyelids lowered even more; his eyes, almost closed, stared at him with a dull sadness.

"You still have a choice, that's no small thing. And it would be very sad if you only realised you'd had a choice when it was already too late. Life is confoundingly short, you can't know that."

"Depends: short for one, long for another."

"Short for everybody. Only a few leave something behind, others – just rotten boards."

"Is that so important? Everyone lives as they see fit and know how."

"It's important that a person doesn't end up standing alone on a platform."

The diesel locomotive raced by quickly, as if it weren't even planning to stop. The conductors stood in each doorway with their signal lamps. Nobody got off, nobody got on. Tired voices yelled to each other up at the front end near the baggage car.

He extended his hand to Aparjods.

"You still have a choice."

Aparjods's moist fingers clenched his hand and didn't let go.

"I don't know if Vilis mentioned it, but when we were in high school we gave an oath to always remain true to who we were and to truth and justice; we signed our promise in blood: 'Better to be naked than to cloak ourselves in lies.' When you're young, it's normal to use powerful words. But do you know why people lie?"

"No."

There was no hope of freeing himself from Aparjods's grasp.

"I didn't know back then either. Back then I thought that lying had to mean fooling others. But that's not true. You can also lie to yourself. And, honestly, those are the worst lies of all, when you try to fool your conscience. Ahhhh, a person knows when they've done wrong, when they've gone with the flow and been cowards, when they've defended the truth that's convenient, when they've pushed someone else off the raft so they can stay dry. It's just that the nakedness of honesty isn't always pleasant. But you want to be able to sleep at night, you want to be without a single wrinkle, like on a retouched photograph."

The official on duty came out of the station and looked at his watch.

"You think I don't know why she didn't come today? I know, I knew yesterday that she wouldn't come, I knew it the day before and the day before that. But tomorrow I'll think of a thousand different reasons to excuse her and excuse myself, while the truth gets pushed out of sight again. Why are you looking at me like a frightened chick? Do you think I'm drunk or don't know what I'm saying? I'm not and I do. I've only been drunk twice in my life: when I had to shoot the old herding dog and when Vilis married your mother; today my head is clearer than clear."

The official on duty lifted his hand.

"Are you getting on?" the train conductor asked in Russian. "The train is leaving."

"Wait, you wanted to know if I was at Vilis's funeral. I wasn't. I was too used to thinking I was better than him. Vilis was always lower, and I was always higher. But back then, when I'd already bought the wreath at the shop, I understood I couldn't bring it myself, because I lacked the will. My legs felt like playing cards and if I hadn't been able to put my weight on something, I'd have fallen over. To suddenly lower yourself when you've always felt like you were on a higher level isn't actually all that easy, and you can't stand by your friend's casket like that, with unsteady legs. Staying up high comes at a price. I told myself I was ill. I even called the doctor and coughed while talking to him on the phone. Now your heart will be at peace. Better be quick about getting on the train. I'm not keeping you. You don't understand what I'm saying anyway."

The wheels began to turn almost imperceptibly. Aparjods let go of his hand and stepped back.

"Please go. This is a very comfortable and convenient train. You'll get a good night's rest before Riga."

There was still a chance to jump on the train. The conductor, standing in the doorway, was saying something to him. Aparjods was also saying something. But he only heard the wail of the locomotive, which was becoming louder, deafening him – and he couldn't move an inch.

The last of the train cars, its red lights shining, dived into the night. The official on duty walked back into the station.

Aparjods, wheezing as he breathed, chuckled quietly.

"I never thought you'd stay."

"Me neither."

"But it's interesting. We can go to the hostel. Your bed is free."

"Thank you."

"I've got some good cognac."

"Thank you."

"We can go sit in the castle ruins at one of the millstone tables."

"Thank you."

"Shall we go?"

"No."

"The next train leaves in three hours. You're not thinking of sitting here at the station, are you?"

"No."

"But what then?"

"That's only my concern. Good night."

The scent of the morning was carried by the wind as it rustled the leaves of the trees.

20

The sun hadn't risen yet, but birdsong was already lively. He was shaking just a little bit, as if he'd fallen asleep in his clothes and only just woken up. His shirt seemed stuck to his back and was damp and crumpled.

Grey newspaper pages fluttered on the benches where they'd been left. In the dim light, the dance floor looked uneven and dirty, rotten boards had been replaced with new ones. A snapped birch tree hung alongside the empty shack containing the refreshment counter.

He walked around the jagged, trampled hedge and climbed up on to the stage. The wind lazily flapped a loose cardboard shingle. He wanted to sit down on the edge of the stage and wait until the sun rose, but he jumped down after all, into the sand, which had already been disturbed by many feet. His footsteps had to be here somewhere too. Also Lība's footsteps. And Kamita's footsteps. Pressed into it like a seal into wax on a historic document. He leaned down and studied the trampled sand for a long time, almost as if he were hoping to find something meaningful in it.

He walked down to the river. His shoes became wet in the dewy meadow and many small blades of grass stuck to them. The spots where campfires had burned were blackened with ashes and charred branches. A barely noticeable mist rose from a brown stream that gurgled quietly as it moved around low-hanging branches and sandy shoals. White foam was collecting along the edges of the bays along with broken bulrushes and greenish algae. He had the feeling of being the only one left in the entire world. The songs of the unseen birds only echoed that emptiness – like the howl of the wind and the hum of bark in a pine tree's branches.

He took off his clothes and stepped into the river. The water felt soft and warm. The sand moved under his feet. And immediately he felt the river's current.

His first few strong arm motions seemed to wake him up, his head grew clearer. He was splashing water everywhere on purpose, joyfully feeling the power of his muscles and his body's agility, he dived into the water and emerged out of it again, loudly pushing out his breath. The current carried him to the side, but he fought to get to the centre of the river.

He climbed out on to the shore just a bit further off from the spot where he'd left his clothes, and ran back on the small path along the riverside, shaking his dripping hair and wiping his shoulders and chest with his palms.

After he'd dressed he noticed his shadow: the sun had risen.

When he returned to town, the sunlight was flowing like a golden stream across his back and over the cobblestone street. A bus went by. A man was walking in front of him whistling, with his hands shoved in his pockets. A waltz from a Lehár operetta was coming from an open window and a woman's voice said, "This is Riga speaking, the correct time is…"

It was still very early. At least an hour too early. Fatigue and missed sleep gradually began to overtake him. But no excuses, no changing his mind or delays. Still an hour left…

The van from the collective farm was bringing potatoes. The caretakers were cleaning the pavement, spraying sparkling streams of water. Crates of milk bottles were unloaded in front of shops. Drowsy men on their way to work stood deep in thought while drinking beer at the kiosk in the market square.

For some reason he thought of the ash-covered spots where the campfires had been; their flames had glowed so beautifully at night, swaying in the darkness like bright water lilies suspended in black water. And the dusty, colourful dance floor, it too was different in his memory. If he'd left earlier…

Likewise, the promises that people make to themselves at night look completely different in the light of day. The truth… Hadn't everything at the campfire with Kamita that night seemed like the truth?

It still didn't really make any sense to him and it kept occupying his thoughts. But none of that mattered anymore. And time just kept on moving forward.

He remembered Old Mārtiņš and his yellow kvass barrel by the station, the freshly washed, wet mugs, the coin dish filled with spillage from each pour, the wide, brown jet of kvass. He needed a drink, his mouth was parched from thirst. Maybe Mārtiņš was already working with the bottles and jugs? He probably was. But then he'd have to pass by that building again. How many times was it now? Back and forth, back and forth. As if he were on a short chain.

But why not? It was most likely all in his imagination.

Passing by the dormitory, he slowed down on purpose. The door opened and three young women came out. For a moment they cast their eyes in his direction. He felt it and blushed. That was all. The women, talking loudly, bustled past him.

It'll be fine. He felt a little better. What was still eating at him? Did he really think that Aparjods was still standing in front of the station? And even if he were standing there, why did it matter?

Mārtiņš was hunched down and working energetically around the vat, what exactly he was doing wasn't clear.

"Good morning."

"Good morning, good morning."

"Is the shop open already?"

"The shop's open, but the barrel's empty. They haven't brought it yet. This time the young hero will have to make do without his power drink."

Catching his breath, he looked more closely at Mārtiņš.

"Why did you call me a hero?"

"A good salesman knows that if he's going to make a mistake, it's better to go too far than not far enough. Going too far is just a simple oversight, but not going far enough – that's like fraud. Would you like it better if I just called you a consumer?"

"That would be closer to the truth."

"Don't hold it against this old-timer, I've been a salesman my whole life. And it's best not to take what a salesman says too seriously. When I was young it was practically a rule: don't skimp on compliments, they don't cost you anything, but might bring you some profit. And you had to remember this too: never try to cheat a customer, people don't like to be cheated. Let them cheat themselves and they'll love it."

"Do you know what time the post office opens?"

"I think at nine. But maybe earlier. I don't have much to do with that institution. Back during the Ulmanis years they opened at eight. But now…"[13]

"Does the telegraph office work all night long?"

"Young man, you'll have to ask that of someone else. I'd probably get it wrong as I've got even less to do with the telegraph office than I do with the post office."

"Thank you."

"Not a problem. Can I pour you some water in a cup? Sure, water doesn't hold a candle to kvass, but if you're very thirsty…"

He drank the water and walked back to the centre.

The post office was still closed, but the telegraph office was open. The air in the gloomy room was pleasantly cool. The recently washed floor exuded a refreshing moistness.

"The forms are on the table," the employee said as she tousled her hair and twisted her lips whilst looking into the mirror she held pressed into her hand.

"Thank you. Perhaps you have stationery and an envelope?"

"With stamps."

---

13   Kārlis Ulmanis: the first prime minister, and returned on to office on four occasion; on the fourth he led a successful coup and continued as prime minister and president of Latvia under the title of *vadonis* (leader) until the country lost its independence following the Soviet occupation in 1940.

For some reason there was a picture of a skier on the envelope. And a high-voltage tower. And a snow-covered spruce.

He sat down at the little table, rubbed the end of the pen against the plastic inkwell and immediately began to write, knowing that the salutation sounded silly and that the pen was tearing the paper in an ugly way, but he didn't stop and didn't correct anything:

Lība, you'll receive this letter only in the event that I'm not able to meet you myself. I can't leave without telling you the truth, it would be sad if you tormented yourself with guilt, believing that you're worse and I'm better than is actually true.

I'm not Aleksandrs Draiska. I should have told you that right from the start, but lies are like quicksand – easy to slip into, but difficult to get out of.

Aleksandrs Draiska and I both served in the same regiment and the same platoon. I had no one to write to and he got letters by the stack. At lunchtime when the man on duty brought the mail, he'd walk around, waving the stack of letters in the air, reading the most interesting ones out loud. I liked your letter and I told him so. 'So, write her back in my place,' he said, 'do you think I need it?'

So, that's how I ended up writing you, half jokingly, half seriously, as soldiers do. I didn't have the courage to give my real name, because you'd sent your letter to a poet, but I was just a regular, unremarkable soldier.

Everything else I wrote you is true. I came to Randava because of you and to find you. And I'm so sorry that it all turned out so differently than I'd hoped or wanted.

Lība, I don't know what will happen with us going forward and I suspect you don't know either. But I understand one thing, which is that if we both went our separate ways, then everything would be too easy and too pitiful. After all, what we've lost are the lies we told each other.

I feel I'll give you this letter even if they let me in to see you, because I doubt I'll have the courage to tell you any of this looking you in the eye.

I'll wait for your answer. The address is on the envelope. Get well soon. Kaspars Krūmiņš

He didn't read the letter a second time, he just blew on it and waved it in the air until the ink dried.

Now that the letter had finally been written, he wanted to get to the hospital as soon as he could.

He walked quickly, as the chill passed through him in waves, much like what he'd felt in the past at school events before he'd walk out on to the stage, or recently in the army when he was waiting for the command to jump during his parachute training. In fact, he was thinking less about actually meeting Lība than about walking into the hospital ward and speaking with the nurse, and there was also something else indefinable and unfathomable, unpleasant and difficult to overcome, which he couldn't exactly envision, but was definitely waiting there for him.

An ambulance had just pulled up and was standing in front of the hospital's doors. The hospital orderlies lifted out a stretcher. There was an unnaturally thin body covered in a blanket on it. An older man and a younger woman wearing house slippers with red silk flowers on them stood around giving orders.

For a moment he was confused and stopped, but then decided that the crowd was actually useful and walked in following the stretcher. Nobody stopped him, nobody asked him anything.

The windows along the sides of the corridor were open. Occasional bursts of coolness from the outside refreshed the sharp, stale air of the hospital.

It wasn't far now. One more turn, just one more. And then the white glass doors.

Suddenly, he realised he felt hot. He passed his hand over his face and down across his neck – torrents of sweat were pouring off of him. He'd prepared himself to encounter the nurse right after opening the door, but there was no one there.

Even better, he thought, thank God.

He rushed ahead. At the end of the hallway he was met with the sound of an old woman's voice behind him: "Young man, where are you going?"

He kept moving.

"Young man..."

It was too late to turn around.

"...where are you going..."

The little room was empty. The folding screen was leaning against the wall. Both beds had been stripped of their linens and mattresses, a cold light reflected from their metallic skeletons.

A nurse came up, not the one he thought he'd meet, but a different one, with a rather pale face and eyes set deep within their dark orbits.

"Where is Lība?"

He couldn't say anything more than that, but he also couldn't be silent. Silence would be too harsh, he had to say something just to keep the silence from setting in.

"Lība Marcinkēviča... tell me, please... she was here... in this bed..."

The dark eyes looked at him with a weary, intolerable gaze.

"Lība Marcinkēviča died last night."

He had no sense of how long he stood in front of this woman. Then he turned towards the hallway that had brought him there and let it slowly take him away.

He stopped at the first window. A harsh, white light was shining through it and the world revealed itself in shocking clarity – a clarity that was more transparent and bare than it had ever been before. Despite everything that had happened, he'd have to live in that world. And he'd have to live in it with an open heart and stay true to his humanity.

1970